E FOR

The Servants' Quarters

NPR Summer 2009 "Critics' List" pick
JVibe "Scintillating Summer Read"

"Freed's great strength as a writer—like Anne Tyler and Muriel
Spark, to name but two—is that she realizes 'normal' is a word
that barely, if ever, applies to human beings in real life, let alone
in serious fiction . . . Freed writes with great clarity and skill, and
her occupancy of Cressida's voice is exemplary."
— *New York Times Book Review*

"The broadest echoes of this wonderfully engaging novel come
from Jane Austen and George Eliot. For this accomplishment
any reader, male or female, wants to wave hat and veil and shout
brava, brava!"—NPR

"*The Servants' Quarters* . . . is written in a most appealing
voice—the wise child in a household of secrets. It's a haunt-
ing voice in literature, the child who will take charge of her own
destiny and will not be told which rooms she can enter, which
she cannot." — *Los Angeles Times*

"Deeply atmospheric, with a high-spirited narrator who fre-
quently endears . . . This is a love story for outsiders, set against
the backdrop of the modern world. As in Charlotte Brontë's
Jane Eyre or Marguerite Duras' *The Lover*, the central figures
compel and seem to deeply belong together, despite conven-
tions."— *San Francisco Chronicle*

The Servants' Quarters

Also by LYNN FREED

The
Servants' Quarters

LYNN FREED

Mariner Books
Houghton Mifflin Harcourt
Boston   New York

For RWK

First Mariner Books edition 2010
Copyright © 2009 by Lynn Freed

For information about permission to reproduce selections
from this book, write to Permissions, Houghton Mifflin
Harcourt Publishing Company, 215 Park Avenue South,
New York, New York 10003.

www.hmhbooks.com

Library of Congress Cataloging-in-Publication Data
Freed, Lynn.
    The Servants' Quarters/Lynn Freed.—1st ed.
        p.   cm.
    ISBN 978-0-15-101288-6
    1. Jewish families—Fiction. 2. Jews—South Africa—Fiction.
3. South Africa—Fiction. 4. Domestic fiction. 5. Jewish fiction.
I. Title.
    PR9369.3.F68S47 2009
    823'.914—dc22
                                2008029152
ISBN 978-0-547-33603-9 (pbk.)

Text set in ITC Galliard Std Roman
Designed by Linda Lockowitz

Printed in the United States of America
DOC 10 9 8 7 6 5 4 3 2 1

Part One

Chapter 1

If every family chooses someone to punish, I was the one chosen by mine. Mr. Harding, for instance. When he came to lunch, Ma always put him next to me. Why me? I wanted to know. Why not Miranda, she's a freak herself? Every night Miranda woke up screaming that the Germans were coming for her over a wall. *War* I kept telling her, it's *war*, not *wall*! But Ma just told me to keep my oar out of it, Miranda had a fixation, she said, and anyway, what would I know about the war, I hadn't even been born until it was over. So it was hopeless. Every Sunday I was stuck next to Mr. Harding, and every night Miranda was allowed to go on screaming until Ma came down the passage with the DDT.

Nightmares and mosquitoes were the only reasons we were allowed to wake Ma up. If it was a nightmare, she'd just switch on all the lights and tell us to go back to sleep. But if it was a mosquito, we had to try to catch it and put it in a matchbox so that the man from the mosquito department could know just which sort it was and where to find its breeding ground— stupid, if you ask me, because the mosquito man himself said they can breed overnight in a wheelbarrow, or an upturned avocado-pear leaf.

At first I thought mosquitoes were the reason Mr. Harding wore a veil over his panama hat. But no, said Ma, he wore the hat because he'd been shot down by the Germans in a ball of fire and had had to drag himself, still burning, to hide behind a wall. It was men like George Harding, she said, who'd won the war for us, and if we thought hiding behind a wall had been the end of it, we'd be quite wrong, because then there'd been operation after operation without benefit of ether, and yet look how cheerful he was! Look how much he loved us children!

But he didn't love us, I could have told her that. I did tell her. I said, "I don't like him, and I hate his voice, and I don't want to sit next to him anymore." What I couldn't tell her was that the war was becoming a terror for me, too—that it had taken the shape of Mr. Harding's scarred, pink, dented head with its freckles, and its false eye, and its sprouts and tufts of hair. Just as I'd be squinting to block out the bad side of it, he'd twist the whole thing around to look down at me and say, "Would you pass the butter please, Cressida?"

When he came to the house, the dogs had to be locked in the sewing room, and even then they went wild at the sight of that hat and veil sailing along the crazy paving. At first he'd worn the hat inside, too, even to the table, and I'd try to keep my eyes on his hands, the way his fork disappeared under the veil without even touching it. His hands themselves were normal— large and straight and strong. As long as you kept looking at them, you could almost forget you had never seen his face.

But then, one day, just as we were settling into the lounge for coffee, a gust from the floor fan lifted the edge of his veil and he made a wild grab for it. The trouble was he grabbed too fiercely and pulled the whole hat askew. So then there he was, staring out at us like a Cyclops, and I turned to Miranda and squinted one eye, sucking in my lips hideously. And she ran out of the room like a baby.

"Oh *George!*" my mother said, trying to cover up. She waved her cigarette and looked straight at him in that way of hers. "Why not just take the hat off? You don't need it here, with us."

He hesitated for a moment, but then he did lift it off. He put it upside down on the arm of his chair, folding the veil neatly inside. Meanwhile, Ma herself couldn't help staring. Everyone was staring, even Miranda from the other side of the French doors. Only Phineas remembered to take the sugar bowl over to him and keep the tongs towards him as he held it out. So why can't you put him in the kitchen with Phineas? I asked Ma as soon as Mr. Harding had left. But she only turned on me as usual. "You're a disgrace!" she said. "Whatever you did to send Miranda out like that! You're a troublemaker! You're a bad seed!"

She'd got the idea of the bad seed from a book she'd read. She often got ideas like this. After she saw *The Children's Hour* at Film Society, she started asking whether Bunch had ever tried to kiss us on the lips. Whatever the case, Ma said, we were not to walk around in the altogether when Bunch was staying, and, if she forgot to take her towel to the bathroom again, we were just to leave it hanging on the doorknob. Never mind that Bunch was mad, never mind that she was our aunt, and old and fat and ugly, almost as ugly as Mr. Harding.

He lived with his mother at Harding's Rest at the top of the hill. It had been built by his grandfather with sugar money, Ma said, and there was a lake in the garden with swans on it, and a grove of fruit trees as well. She loved words like "lake" and "grove" for anything the Hardings had, but I'd seen the garden through a gap in the hedge, and there wasn't a lake there at all, just a pond with a flock of hadedahs pecking around it. There wasn't a grove either. It was a measly stand of mango trees, with monkeys screaming out of them, and mangos rotting on the ground.

Ma had been up to Harding's Rest only once, during the war. A troopship had stopped in South Africa on its way to Suez, and old Mrs. Harding had gone down to the docks herself to invite the soldiers up to the house for a party—never mind officers only, never mind four men to one woman for a change. The Hardings were old school, Ma said, a dying breed that didn't stay home playing golf when the world was in a crisis. They mucked in, gave parties for men going off to die. The men themselves had toiled up the hill in rickshaws, or just trudged all the way on foot. And such laughter there'd been! Such dancing in the moonlight! Such a supper laid out in the grand hall!

But then Mr. Harding had come down in his ball of fire, and his older brother ran off to the war and got himself killed. And so that was that for parties, and also for old Mrs. Harding's sanity, because why had she bothered to have sons in the first place if they were just going to be burned up and shot down? By the time Mr. Harding came home in his hat and veil, she'd taken to running out into the road with the silver, giving it to any old native who happened to be passing by. One day, she gave Phineas two forks and a serving spoon, and he brought them straight home to Ma. So up she went to give them back. But the housekeeper who answered the door was barely civil, just snatched them back as if Ma had stolen them herself.

And it wasn't until Mr. Harding rang the doorbell months and months later that Ma realised how old school the Hardings really were. He'd just heard what had happened to my father, he said—they'd been trying to keep him from unfortunate things, which was rather unforgivable under the circumstances, but thank you for bringing the cutlery back, and if there was anything he could do, she need only ask, and so forth.

My father had known the Hardings before he'd even met Ma. They'd all been at Cambridge together, and when they'd come back they'd played golf at the Royal Country Club. My father had only been asked to join in the first place, Ma said, because he was the better sort of Jew. And from the way she said it, I thought that she herself must be a worse sort of Jew, which was probably the better thing to be in the end, because one day my father had been hit on the head by a golf club, and ever since then he'd been lying in his corner room, and Phineas had to feed and change him like a baby. And all that had happened only two months before I was even born.

Miranda was the only one who would tell me what my father had been like when he was normal, but first she had to look around to see if Ma could hear her. Miranda was dead scared of Ma. She was dead scared of me, too, although she was six and a quarter years older than I was. Once, when she'd left her secret drawer open by mistake, I found a photo of my father and her at the beach. She was on a pony, and he was standing next to her with one hand on the reins and the other at her waist to steady her. I stared at that hand, wanting badly to have it for myself. So I stole the photo and hid it under the house, where Miranda was scared to go, and when she found that it was missing, she couldn't even tell Ma, because how could she have got that photo in the first place? All the albums were locked in the linen cupboard. Dwelling on the past would bring us nothing but grief, Ma said. We should take a leaf out of her book. Did she dwell on the past? Did she pine after a chimera?

Still, she herself kept a photograph of my father in a silver frame on the hi-fi. He was leaning forward, resting his chin on his hand, with a cigarette between his fingers, and a thin moustache. Every night she lifted her glass of brandy and ginger ale and said, Chin-chin! And when I asked why she never went up to his room to say Chin-chin! to him personally, she just said, What would be the point? He wouldn't know her from Phineas.

But he did know. Phineas said you could tell by the fingers. He always laid my father's arms over the sheet so that he could watch his fingers. They were smooth and square and dark, nothing like Mr. Harding's, and sometimes I liked to hold them, just to think of what it would be like to hold a normal father's hand. And sometimes, when Phineas wasn't there, I'd lift the sheet to see what was going on underneath. But it was always the same—a smooth, dark body with a nappy pinned around it like an Indian's. If I smelled the nappy, I had to ring for Phineas to come and change him. And then he'd chase me out because I wasn't allowed to watch.

There were a lot of things in my father's room I wasn't supposed to look at—his silk dressing gown with the hanky in the pocket, his smoking jacket still smelling of cigars, and then, right at the back of the wardrobe, two concentration-camp books in a brown paper packet. I found them anyway, of course, and took them out and looked at them. And soon Phineas was reading them as well. He would sit on the stool, moving his finger across the page, and then look up and say, "Hau, those bad peoples, Miss Cress! Hau, hau, hau!"

And the mad thing was that Mr. Harding himself must have given Ma the books in the first place, because in front of each was written TO MW FROM GH in dark blue ink. Inside were pictures of naked bodies heaped into piles, and also naked men just standing there, naked women too. I told Miranda all this, and sometimes I smuggled a book out to show her. She was allowed to wear lipstick now, and high heels, and often a boy would phone to ask her to the pictures or the ice rink. I told her that Germans made girls like her lie naked on beds all day whether they liked it or not, and what's more, if she woke them up with her nightmares, she'd be off to the gas chamber in a minute.

"Miranda's crying again," I said to my father, "and I'm going to get the blame as usual."

He never answered, of course; he never even moved his fingers for me. Still, if he'd been a real father, he'd probably have given me a scolding. So maybe it was better this way, although I longed for him to look up just once and say, You're right, I'll tell Ma she has to say she's sorry.

And then one day, when I was in his room, the doorbell rang and Bunch made a mad dash for it. She was down for the Christmas holidays and had forgotten, as usual, that she wasn't supposed to answer the door. Bunch loved answering the door. It gave her a chance to pretend the house was still her own, and to ask people into the lounge for tea, even if it was only the man from the mosquito department. Forgot? My toe! Ma said. Bunch was bent on making a spectacle of herself, and if she started up again at the table with "Is this a dagger that I see before me?" I was not even to *think* of joining in with my own knife or she'd have Phineas remove my place to the kitchen for the duration of the visit.

"Mr. Harding!" I cried. He was backed up against the

front door, shouting "DOWN! DOWN!" although it made no difference, of course. The dogs were in a frenzy over the hat, jumping, barking, growling.

"Help!" Bunch squeaked. She was crouched out of sight, on the other side of the kist, holding the brass pestle at the ready.

Mr. Harding was thrashing hard now with his riding crop, shouting, "DOWN! DOWN, I SAY!" But the minute he hit one dog, the other would latch on to a trouser leg, and, in all the twisting and thrashing, his hat fell off, and Scylla got hold of it, shaking it by the veil as if it were a cat.

I grabbed her collar and dragged her into the pantry, then went back for Circe. "Here," I said, panting, handing him back his hat.

He twisted around quickly to look down at me, his whole head roaring red, even the good eye. "Those dogs are a menace!" he shouted. "I have a good mind to have them put down!"

But who'd asked him to the house in the first place, I wanted to know? He only ever came when he was invited, and he was never invited when Bunch was with us.

"Where's your mother?" he demanded, slamming the hat back onto his head. But it looked more ridiculous than ever because it was bashed and bitten now, with bits of veil hanging around it like a cobweb.

Bunch scrambled up and made a mad dash for the kitchen, still hanging on to the pestle.

"That's my aunt," I said. "She works as an usherette."

He looked down at me then with a twist of his head. "How old are you now, Cressida?"

"Nine and three quarters."

"Ah yes!" he said, as if I'd given him the right answer. "There's going to be a boy about your age coming to live at Harding's Rest and he'll need someone to play with."

I nodded, even though Harding's Rest terrified me almost as much as the war. A boy there would only make things worse.

"And here"—he took a thick envelope out of his pocket—"make sure that your mother receives this as soon as she comes home please. Are the dogs properly secured? Good!"

Chapter 2

As it turned out, we all had to move up to Harding's Rest as soon as we could pack up our own house. The trouble was money, Ma said. We'd run out of it completely, and so the house had to be sold to pay off the bank. What's more, Ma would have to take a job as a florist or a shop assistant, and Miranda would have to go to the government school because there wasn't a hope of a scholarship or a bursary for her. Not that mine amounted to that much, mind you—it paid for my school fees and uniforms—but, as for Miranda, she was destined to become a shorthand typist if she was lucky, and frankly, Ma said, she was heartily sick of the lot of us.

I watched her light a cigarette, trying to imagine her arranging flowers. She'd won the senior English and needlework prizes at school, and had chosen *Shakespeare: The Complete Works* for one, and *The Iliad* and *The Odyssey* in their own box for the other. She kept them on top of the piano to remind herself of what she might have amounted to if my father hadn't come along with his imploring ways. As it was, she'd been swept off her feet when she was barely out of school, put in this tomb of a house, tied down with two children, and now look—a grass widow at thirty-five. Ha-ha she didn't think.

So why can't Miranda just go out and *be* a shorthand typist? I said. Then Ma herself wouldn't have to be a florist, and we wouldn't have to go and live with Mr. Harding. But Ma just told me to keep my clever ideas to myself, who did I think I was, Madame Curie? And anyway, we weren't going to be living *with* Mr. Harding, we were going to be inhabiting the carriage house at the far end of his driveway. Family retainers had lived there in the olden days, she said, but now the real servants' quarters were behind the big house, and as soon as the carriage house was cleaned and painted, we'd be moving out of this white elephant she'd been saddled with as a bride and living according to our means for a change.

"We're going to be in their old servants' quarters up there," I said to my father, watching his fingers for a sign. "And I don't see why we have to."

His eyes were open as usual, staring at the top of the wardrobe.

"It's all very well for you," I said. "You'll just go on lying wherever they put you. I'm the one who's going to have to play with Mr. Harding's boy, and I don't see why he even wants to save us in the first place!"

When I'd tried to find out from Ma, she'd just said there were *some* men who took responsibility and came forward when they heard one was about to consign one's life to a cheap little flat on the beachfront, *some* men who didn't spend their time playing golf and building air-raid shelters while others were going off to die.

"And she's blaming you for it as well," I said to my father. "And I'd rather live on the beachfront any day."

"Why you so naughty?" said Phineas, coming in with my father's supper. He had a way of creeping up on his bare feet that always gave me a fright. "Why you don't do homework? You want to be stupid like Miranda?"

I huffed down into the chair. Phineas thought he was a member of the family, older and better than anyone else. He'd come to work for us long before I was born, when he couldn't even read a recipe. So Ma had sent him to night school, thinking he'd stop when he could read recipes. But now he was up to standard four, and if we didn't look out he'd take driving lessons on the q.t., she said, and get a job as a driver, and that would be the final blow, wouldn't it?

"Out now," he said, stuffing pillows behind my father. He never allowed me to stay when my father was being fed. "Out now, food it's getting cold."

But when I came downstairs, grumbling about Phineas, Ma just took his side. He was a Zulu of the old school, she said, he took pride in his work, pride in our family, too. Sometimes, when she forgot how cross she was with my father, she'd take pride in him as well. He'd always been a cut above, she'd say, a man of principle who wouldn't even buy a German camera.

But I was sick of it. However wonderful everything had been before I was born, we weren't much better than servants ourselves now. "So now we're a cut below?" I said.

Ma didn't believe in slapping. It was what common people did, she said, people who didn't know any better. But suddenly now her hand flew out and slapped me hard across the cheek. At first we were both so surprised that we just stared at each other. Then I felt the tears rising in my throat, and out they came in big, gasping sobs.

"Oh darling," she said, pulling me to her. "I'm so sorry, but you can't possibly understand what I'm going through." She laid her cheek on my head and stroked my hair.

"Ma," I said, still heaving, "please don't make me play with that boy."

"What?"

"I mean, why can't Miranda play with him? Why's it always got to be me?"

She pushed me away, and I stepped back in case she decided to slap me again. But she didn't. She just folded her arms and narrowed her eyes and then shouted so loudly that even my father must have been able to hear. "Selfish!" she shouted. "One little thing Mr. Harding asks and it's too much trouble! Selfish!" she shouted again. "Ruthless, too! You are selfish, and you are ruthless, and you'll go far in life, my girl!"

I ran out, and down to my room, sat at my desk, and wrote the words out before I could forget them. Then I tore out the page and folded it smaller and smaller, and sealed it up with sticky tape, and put it into my pocket. For a whole week I kept touching it there like a lucky charm, and when it got washed with my uniform by mistake it didn't matter after all, because I knew the words by heart and could write them out any time I wanted to: You are selfish, and you are ruthless, and you'll go far in life, my girl.

Chapter 3

As soon as our books were arranged on shelves, I looked up "carriage house" in the encyclopedia because I couldn't work out how even a small carriage could ever have fitted into the place we were in.

"Mr. Harding gypped us!" I said to my father. "It's not a carriage house, it's a stable! And we have to sleep in the servants' quarters upstairs! And he made us give the dogs away even though they never actually bit him, just his trousers and his stupid hat! And I hate him! I really and truly HATE him!"

"*Hate* it's a bad word," said Phineas, coming in with my tea.

When I came home from school, he brought me tea in my father's room now, which was really just one of the stables, on the far side of the kitchen. All the downstairs rooms had been stables once, even the kitchen itself, Ma said, but Mr. Harding had put doors between them, and knocked two into one for a lounge/dining room, and built a skinny verandah all around the outside. Upstairs were our bedrooms, where the old retainers used to sleep. There were bars on the windows because they looked right out over the back lane, which one might consider picturesque, Ma said, if one were on the Continent.

But we weren't on the Continent, we were against the back wall of Harding's Rest, with a passageway running right under my bedroom to the back gate. And so every time someone wanted to come in or go out there'd be bells ringing, and servants calling out, and then a clanging open and a crashing shut, and worst of all was the awful silence afterwards. It was no good calling for Ma, she was down at the far end of the corridor next to Miranda. And so there I lay, staring into the dark and trying to remember that I hadn't even been born during the war. But it made no difference. Every night the Germans came climbing up the wall anyway, cutting through the bars of my windows as if they were made of string.

Phineas was the only one who listened to my troubles. When I told him about the gate, he said he'd ask the big-house servants to let him answer it himself. Mr. Harding had told us all to come in through the front gate if we wanted to, but I preferred the long way around, up Montpelier, along Cadogen, and down the lane to the back gate. And when Phineas came to let me in, I didn't even have to ask before he said, "The boy he's not come yet."

I went to sit in the wicker chair next to my father's bed. His skin gleamed from the aloe Phineas rubbed on for mosquito bites. Phineas had his own DDT spray now, but it did no good. As soon as you opened a door or a window, in they came from the stand of wild bananas on the other side of the courtyard wall. Ma must ask Mr. Harding to chop them down,

Phineas said, and please to ask her again for that special stuff
from the chemist because my father was itchy even though he
couldn't scratch. Phineas himself had asked her twice already,
but since we'd come up to Harding's Rest, she'd lost interest
in mosquitoes, she was always too busy with the shop.

The Cotton Reel had been Mr. Harding's idea. He was the
one who'd given Ma the money to buy it. It was a loan, she
said, an investment in her future, although how on earth she
was supposed to make good on spools of cotton and skeins of
wool she'd like someone to tell her. Only Miranda seemed to
warm to the whole arrangement. Every afternoon she caught
the bus from the government school and took over at the
counter until it was time to go home. She'd found her niche in
haberdashery, Ma said, just look how happy it made her when
customers came asking especially for her.

And so Miranda was the one Mr. Harding had really saved.
She'd even given up her fixation, and nothing I could do
would make her run screaming to Ma anymore. On the very
first night, Ma had left her door open because there were no
fanlights in the bedrooms and the walls were as thick as a pris-
on's, she said. And then, the next morning at breakfast, she
was so proud of Miranda for not waking up screaming that I
couldn't bear to tell her the Germans had just moved down
the passage to me now.

On Phineas's afternoon off, I had to take the bus to the shop
myself, and sit at the counter to do my homework. But it was
hard to do homework when Miranda was telling people about
knitting needles and sizing a pattern. Ma grumbled that she was
also talking customers into buying cotton instead of sheen, and
showing them how to make do with a cheaper lining.

Only when fine ladies came in did Ma come out of the
back and take over herself. And then soon she'd be leaning

over the counter and dropping her voice so that she could mention Harding's Rest, and wasn't it a crying shame, she'd say, the whole place was going to rack and ruin these days?

So one day I just looked up and said, "But Ma, you were only in the big house that once, during the war." It was true. Except for that party in the moonlight, she'd only ever got as far as the front door. Even after we'd moved up there and she'd found old Mrs. Harding singing under the wild bananas and led her back, struggling and objecting, to the kitchen door—even then no one had asked her in. In fact, Ma said, that dreadful housekeeper hadn't even realised the old woman was on the loose. *Phineas* could give her cards and spades in nursing, she said, although she'd keep that little bit of information to herself, thank you very much. All she needed was for him to take it into his head to better himself and look for a job as a nurse. That would send her right off the deep end, and then where would that land the two of us? That's what she wanted to know.

"Tokyo Rose!" she hissed at me as soon as the ladies were gone. "Viper in the nest! What are you hoping to achieve? To humiliate me even further?"

All the way home she shouted on about humiliation, and then, when we got in, she just grabbed *The Iliad* and charged off, down to Mr. Harding's summerhouse, staying out until it was already dark.

*

"Dad," I said, "Ma's making me have my birthday party in their summerhouse. And what if Mr. Harding comes down there? What if they think he's my father?"

Phineas looked up from *The Scourge of the Swastika*. "Hawu!" he said. "Who going to think that? You just say, 'Hello, Mr. Harding,' then they know. See?"

I huffed down. I couldn't bear the thought of Mr. Harding at my party, whoever they thought he was. "Why can't we just have the party in Jameson Park like other poor people?" I asked Ma at supper. But she just told me to try my provocations elsewhere, she had the size of them now, they were nothing to her.

"Dad," I said, "what if that boy comes before Sunday? I'll just have to run away."

Phineas gave one of his gleeful laughs. "Where you run to? Who they going to look after you when you gone?"

And just then the doorbell rang, and it was a servant from the big house, bringing an envelope.

"Here," said Phineas. "For you."

I folded my arms. "I don't want it."

"Don't be naughty. Here. Open."

I looked at my father. "I won't!"

So Phineas opened it and read it out slowly and carefully.

Dear Cressida,
My nephew, Edgar Harding, will be arriving tomorrow. It would please me if you could come to the house for tea on Friday at four o'clock.
George Harding

"I have netball."

"Netball it's Thursday. Don't be naughty now."

"But it's not fair!" I jumped out of the chair and went to stand next to my father. "And it's all your fault! And I won't go! And they can't make me go! It's not FAIR!"

Chapter 4

The housekeeper must have been waiting on the other side of the door because, just as I was about to bang the knocker, she opened it, peering down at me along her nose like a stork. "Ah!" she said. "There you are!" She pulled me in and closed the door behind me. "I'm Mrs. Arbuthnot. Follow me, please."

But I couldn't follow. Something enormous was staring down at me from the landing. It had eyes and fur and a spear gleaming in the dark.

"Ah yes!" she said, turning around. "Edgar took fright as well." She switched on a light. "There! See? Only a carving."

I looked all around me. The hall was full of carvings. Some were of Zulu warriors, and some of Zulu women in beads and headdresses. There were skins on the floor and elephant tusks over the banisters. Kudu horns and a lion's head with gleaming yellow eyes hung on one wall. The whole place smelled of them, dark and old and horrible. A massive kist stood on the other side of the staircase. It was even bigger than ours, and had huge clawed feet. Anything could have been hiding in it, waiting to lift the lid and jump out at me. I backed towards the door because Mr. Harding himself could have been there. He could have been standing in any dark corner and you wouldn't even have known it.

Mrs. Arbuthnot took hold of my arm. "Come along, please," she said, pushing me across the hall and through some French doors at the far end. Outside was a long pillared verandah with a table laid for tea. A boy was sitting there, and old Mrs. Harding as well, and when Mrs. Arbuthnot led me over, they didn't even look up or smile.

"Aren't we saying hello today, dear?" she said to old Mrs. Harding. "This is Cressida. She's come to play with Edgar."

Old Mrs. Harding twisted herself away with a loud sniff. She was tiny and grey, with her hair pulled back into a bun, and long, drooping ears.

"Ah well, never mind. Edgar, this is Cressida. Stand up and say hello properly, please."

But Edgar wouldn't listen to her either. He just stared down into his lap with his neck and ears flaming. He was small and thin and freckled, with wiry arms and wiry black hair shaved up from the bottom of his head, and if they made me ask him to my party, I would refuse to go myself.

Suddenly old Mrs. Harding leaned over and said, "You come and sit over here, next to me."

But Mrs. Arbuthnot stepped between us, taking the chair herself. "Now we know this is my place, don't we, dear?" she said to old Mrs. Harding. "Cressida, you sit over there, next to Edgar."

I was glad now that I'd worn my dungarees and sandals.

For a moment, standing outside the front door, I'd thought that maybe Ma had been right, I should have worn a dress. But when I'd come home from school and seen that she'd laid out my taffeta gingham and crocheted socks, I just pulled on what I always wore, and didn't bother to put a clip in my hair either. Even Phineas had smiled when I came down the stairs. "You a bad girl," he'd said, shaking his head. "What they going to think over there at that big smart house, hey?"

I sat where I'd been told to, but I wouldn't look at Edgar. I wouldn't look at Mrs. Arbuthnot either. I just stared out into the garden, trying to imagine soldiers dancing in the moonlight and supper tables laid out. But it was impossible. Except for the summerhouse and the pond, it was just an ordinary garden, with ordinary lawns and ordinary flower beds, and a garden boy with a hose, watering the flowers.

"I'll be mother," said Mrs. Arbuthnot, pouring the tea. "Here, Cressida, don't spill now."

But before I could take my saucer, old Mrs. Harding had grabbed Mrs. Arbuthnot's arm, making her spill all over the cloth. "Housemaid's tea!" she said. "How many times do you have to be told? Tea first, milk second!"

I laughed, I couldn't help it. I even looked at Edgar to see if he was laughing. But he wasn't, he was crying. Tears were running down his cheeks and onto his shirt. "Something's the matter with Edgar," I said.

"Ignore him, please," said Mrs. Arbuthnot, arranging the teapot out of old Mrs. Harding's reach. She cut three thin slices of cake and handed them around. Then she cut a fourth, a large one, and put it on a plate and said, "I am going to make sure that Mr. Harding has his tea."

"Good riddance to bad rubbish," mumbled old Mrs. Harding with her mouth full already.

"Something's the matter with Edgar," I whispered to her. He was shuddering as if he had a temperature, and his cup was shaking in the saucer.

But she just bent over her cake, forking it rudely into her mouth.

"How old are you?" I whispered to Edgar.

He turned away, wiping his nose along his arm.

"Here! Girl!" said old Mrs. Harding, reaching for the cake knife. "Would you pass it to me, please?"

"Shall I cut a piece for you?"

"Yes, yes! Quick!"

I jumped up and ran around to her side, but just as I'd got hold of the knife, Mrs. Arbuthnot was back in the doorway. "What do you *think* you're doing?" she shouted.

I dropped the knife and it clattered to the floor.

"For your information," she said to me, picking the knife up and wiping it on her serviette, "Mrs. Harding has a condition. We all have to keep an eye on her sugar."

"Condition! Condition!" grumbled old Mrs. Harding. "She doesn't give a tinker's cuss about anyone's condition! All she wants is Charles. Would you tell him that for me, girl? Would you?"

Charles? I looked at Edgar, but he was just staring, not even eating his cake. The garden boy was pushing a lawn mower now, and there was the smell of grass, and of frangipanis, and when one of the dogs came to put his head on my lap, wanting some cake, it all seemed so normal that I forgot for a moment where I was, where I had to go back to.

"We do *not* feed the dogs at the table!" Mrs. Arbuthnot said. "Out!" she shouted at the dogs. "Shoo!"

I could see she hated dogs. She was probably rude to servants, too. English people like her were always rude to servants, Ma said, always glad to have someone else to look down on.

Old Mrs. Harding began to push herself up. "I'm going to speak to Charles," she said. "He should know what's going on out here."

I stood up too. "I have to go home," I said quickly. "My mother says I have to do my homework."

"Will everyone kindly *sit down* until tea is over," Mrs. Arbuthnot said, pushing old Mrs. Harding down quite rudely. "And don't you think," she said, turning to me, "that it would be polite to wait till tea is over? Don't you think you should go and say good-bye and thank you to Mr. Harding before running off back to your quarters?"

*

Mr. Harding's study was even darker than the hall. It smelled of tobacco and dogs and furniture polish, and there were skins on the floor there, too, and pillows made out of skins, bookshelves all around, and the sun from the Venetian blinds striping across everything.

He sat in a big leather armchair, wearing his hat and veil. "Ah, Cressida!" he said, putting his pipe down and holding out his hand for me to shake.

This was new. Mr. Harding never shook hands at our house. He kept them to himself, as if they were scarred like the rest of him.

"I hear it's your birthday on Saturday," he said. "I have a present for you. Over there."

I turned to look, although I'd seen it on the way in. "I've got a bike already," I said.

"Where are your manners, girl?" Mrs. Arbuthnot barked,

shoving me forward. She would have hit me if she could have, I knew that, but she just held on to my shoulder as if I might run away.

"That will be all, Mrs. Arbuthnot," he said. "Thank you."

"Thank you very much anyway," I mumbled as soon as she was gone.

Mr. Harding leaned forward to tap out his pipe in an ash-tray made out of an elephant's foot. It still had its toenails and wrinkled skin, and he looked like a lampshade, leaning over it like that. Phineas said the servants could tell everything from Mr. Harding's head. If they hadn't fed the dogs on time or old Mrs. Harding came disturbing him in his study, out he would come without his hat, his whole head on fire. And then, ai, they'd all have to watch out!

"Edgar has a matching bike," he said. "But he doesn't yet know how to ride. So perhaps you would accept the gift for my sake? We could keep it over here if you like, and you could keep your own there. How would that be?"

I turned to look out of the window, pressing my lips to-gether. All I could think now was that when you didn't have money, anyone could just come down the road and tell you where you had to live, whether you liked it or not. Tonight the Germans would be coming up the wall again, and there was nothing I could do about it. War! I kept saying to my-self, it's *war*, not wall! But nothing helped. Germans were al-ways climbing up the wall now, it was easy for them. And there would never be anyone to help me, nowhere for me to hide.

Chapter 5

I could make Edgar talk only when Mrs. Arbuthnot wasn't there, and even then it was usually to answer, never to ask. Where's your mother? Don't know. Your father? Don't know. Why did you come here? Uncle. Is he your real uncle? Shrug. Are you scared of him? Shrug. And me? Are you scared of me, too?

He kept his eyes on me as if I might suddenly jump up at him like one of the dogs. When they came barking in, he would run behind a chair, waiting for Mr. Harding to shout "Down! Down!" until the dogs put their ears back and cowered, grinning up at the riding crop.

When I asked Ma if Mr. Harding used the crop on Edgar as well, she said, "Don't be ridiculous, that child has had enough in his life to contend with."

"What?" I asked. "What?"

But she just dragged on her cigarette holder. "You have

any number of friends," she said. "Why do you have to keep charging over there?"

"I don't keep charging," I said. "Mr. Harding asks me to go."

And what could she say to this? She was always reminding us that we owed our lives to men like Mr. Harding, and, now that he had saved us from a cheap little flat on the beachfront, how could she tell me not to go over if he wanted me to? Anyway, she was always on the lookout for him herself, grabbing one of her books as soon as she came home from the shop, and then making off with it across the garden and down to the summerhouse, where she knew he liked to sit and read in the late afternoon.

Once, when I was creeping up behind the bamboo, I heard Mr. Harding say, "But I warned you, my dear, did I not warn you that everything would change after you came up here? Did I not make that quite clear?" And she jumped to her feet so quickly that I hardly had time to duck down before she'd grabbed *The Iliad* and taken off across the lawn without even saying good-bye to him. I stayed where I was, breathing softly, until he left and went up to the house.

*

"Ma," I said, "Edgar is even slower than Miranda." It was almost fun scolding him as if I were a teacher. I wanted to spank him as well. There were all sorts of things I kept thinking of doing to him.

She fixed me with one of her warning looks. "You have to make allowances for Edgar," she said. It was what Mr. Harding said, too. When I told him that Edgar wouldn't learn how to use the brakes, and kept riding into the pond, and then would run off crying to the house, all sopping wet, leaving me to bring the bikes back—when I told him anything about Edgar, he just gave me a look and said, "Cressida, I'd like you to make allowances for him. Would you do that for me? Would you?"

"But why?" I said to Ma. "Why should I make allowances?"

"Because however peculiar our family might be, it is still a family. Edgar has only Mr. Harding."

"But *why?*"

She clicked her tongue and picked up her *McCall's Magazine*. "What about Ruth Frank? She's just across the road. Why don't you make a friend of her and stop this whining? It doesn't suit you at all."

So it was hopeless. Everything about Mr. Harding seemed to be a secret, even Edgar. When Mrs. Arbuthnot had tried to lead him down to the summerhouse for my birthday party because I'd been forced to invite him after all, he'd cried and struggled so loudly that, for once, she had to let him have his own way and go back into the house.

I explained to the other girls how everyone forced me to make allowances for him, and that I was the one who was supposed to teach him to ride a bike. But even though they said, "Shame, poor you!" I could tell they thought me peculiar for being at Harding's Rest in the first place. And then, suddenly, there was Mr. Harding himself in his hat and veil, standing on the top lawn and looking down at us like a ghost. When they saw him, they all moved off in a group to the far corner of the summerhouse, leaving me to stand and wave back at him by myself.

And maybe that is when I knew once and for all that I would never be normal like them, not in a hundred years. Even if we hadn't had to sell our house and move up the hill, still there'd be my father lying in his room like a secret himself.

So why shouldn't I just charge over when I had nothing else
to do? Anything was better than being stuck in the old servants' quarters with a peculiar family. It wasn't my fault that
we weren't normal. Nothing that would happen afterwards
would be my fault either, although Ma would go to the ends
of the earth to blame it all on me, and on Mr. Harding, and on
my father as well.

Chapter 6

"Aren't they ever going to send that boy to school?" Ma said. "Doesn't he have anything better to do than learn to ride a bicycle?" Everything about Edgar annoyed her now, especially the way I could go over to the big house to play with him whenever I felt like it. "If they're going to use you as a nursemaid, the least they could do is to pay you." She stared at herself in the hall mirror. "Gugh!" she said. "One of these days I'm just going to walk away from all this. *Fly* away! Leave the whole bloody lot of you behind!"

I slipped out while she was still staring and found Edgar in the driveway, just outside the courtyard gate. He was always out there, pretending to collect stones. "I can fly, you know," I said. It was easy to boast to Edgar because even though he put his hands in his pockets and shook his head, I could see that he believed whatever I told him.

He shook his head, keeping his eyes on me to see what I'd do next.

So I led him back to the big house, in through the kitchen, and up the back stairs to the landing window. Everyone was resting after lunch, even the servants. I slipped out of my sandals and climbed onto the sill.

In our old house, I had often climbed to the top of the flamboyant and then jumped across onto the roof. Ma said I refused to think of the consequences of anything, and that one day I'd take the whole family down with me, right into the fiery pit. But if you thought of the consequences while you were jumping, you'd fall. I knew that without even knowing that I knew it. So how could I ever explain it to her?

"Look!" I said to Edgar. "Watch me!"

"Don't!" he whispered. "Don't jump!"

I lifted my arms and waved them around like wings. "Watch me fly!" I said. And then I leaped from the windowsill out into the air, falling so quickly that it wasn't like flying at all, it was more like dropping, thumping hard onto the grass, and then rolling and rolling until I could stop and stretch my arms and legs out wide like a star. "See?" I shouted up to him. "See? Now you try!"

He stared down at me and shook his head.

"Go on! It's easy! Just climb onto the sill and jump!"

The upstairs window flew open and Mrs. Arbuthnot leaned out. "What is all this shouting about?" she shouted. "Cressida, what are you doing on the laundry lawn?"

"We're jumping."

"You're what? Where?"

I pointed to the window, and there he was, bending over the sill, looking down at me like a frightened rabbit.

"EDGAR!" she screamed. "EDGAR! Don't you DARE!

You just STAY where you are! I'm coming down to get you."

But that was a stupid thing to say because Edgar was more scared of her than he was of jumping. So, the next thing, he was up on the sill, crouching there, hanging on for dear life.

"Edgar! Edgar!" she shouted, running through the house. "WAIT! STOP!"

And then all at once he jumped, his arms and legs curled in like a spider's, and landed half on the grass, half on the path.

"Are you all right?" I said, sitting up. "Edgar?"

He didn't move, just lay there quite still, with his eyes closed.

I scrambled to my feet, wondering whether to make a dash for it before Mrs. Arbuthnot got there. But it was too late. She was already running out of the kitchen and around the path, screaming, "EDGAR! Jesus Christ! Edgar?" She crouched over him, waved her hand in front of his face. Then she put her ear next to his mouth. "He's breathing! Oh, Jesus, thank you, Jesus, he's breathing!" She lifted his arm. "OH!" she screamed. "Oh NO!"

"What is the matter out here?" Mr. Harding was on the kitchen path now, with his whole head a roaring fire.

"He jumped!" Mrs. Arbuthnot shrieked. She pointed at me. "*SHE* led him to it! SHE is to blame for this!"

"Mrs. Arbuthnot!" he barked. "Calm yourself, please! Is the boy all right?"

"His arm is broken!" she wailed. "Just look at it!"

"Then we must have it set. What else?"

"How would *I* know what else? His insides could be mangled for all I know!"

Mr. Harding came up the steps onto the lawn. "Edgar, are your insides mangled?"

Edgar began to snivel, and Mrs. Arbuthnot set up her shrieking again.

"Mrs. Arbuthnot!" Mr. Harding said. "I shall not ask you again! Kindly pull yourself together! Right now! Good. Now go and call for the driver. Tell him to take you and Edgar to Parklands. I'll have Slatkin meet you there. Cressida, you will come with me."

*

"Well," he said, settling himself into his study chair, "kindly explain what was going on out there."

I didn't look up. Whatever Ma said, it was impossible to look him in the eye when there was only one that worked properly. "I'm sorry," I mumbled, trying to concentrate on the stripes of the zebra skins.

"Sorry about what?"

"Making Edgar jump."

Suddenly, he broke into a roaring laugh. "Tosh! Sit down over there. Sit down, please!"

I sat carefully on the edge of the chair opposite. I wanted to be able to run if I had to.

"Do you know, Cressida, that I have been watching you for most of your ten years?" He laughed again. "It's been like watching a rogue cub upsetting the pride."

I stared at his hands. They were resting like huge paws themselves on the arms of the chair.

"Cressida, Cressida, Cressida! Do you realise that I am the way I am because I was showing off?"

I looked up. "How?" I said. It was the first time I had asked him anything except whether he wanted his coffee black or white.

"I was new at the game, didn't understand it wasn't a game

at all. Every night we went out, and when someone didn't come back, it just seemed at first to be an absence. At first. By the time I didn't come back myself, they all knew what to assume."

Suddenly I remembered that Mr. Harding was there, too, in the night. He was there with the Germans, standing around my bed, and he was the one who always told them I was only pretending to be dead.

"When you fly, you cannot afford to show off," he went on. "When there's a war on, showing off is nothing short of criminal."

"Will Edgar die?"

"Well, if he doesn't, I'd like you to promise you'll do it again."

"Pardon me?"

"Not jump out of windows, of course—you're damned lucky you weren't sliced in half by one of the washing lines, both of you. No. What I would like, Cressida, is for you to make him wild and daring." He leaned forward and pointed his good eye at me. "Wipe him clean of the past! Burn it out of him!"

I nodded as if I knew what he was talking about.

He ran one hand over his head, smoothing down the tufts. "Would you take my request more seriously if I were to remunerate you for your efforts?"

I stared straight at him now. "I beg your pardon?"

"And do stop begging for pardon! What are you hoping to be pardoned for?" He cocked his head.

My own face was reddening now, my throat tightening as usual.

"Here——" He reached into an inside pocket and pulled out some money, already clipped together and folded. "This is my first contribution to our little bargain."

I clasped my hands between my legs and looked away, trying to remember normal things. But nothing could make this seem normal, nothing.

"Not like you to be coy," he said, putting the money on the ashtray between us. "Isn't there something you'd like to save up for?"

I shook my head. All I wanted was to have things the way they'd been before: Mr. Harding up here and us down there in our own house.

"Well, run along then. We'll take this up again when—if—Edgar comes back in one piece."

*

When I got home, Phineas was fussing with my father's pills. Only he knew which one was for what and why. When they ran out, it was Phineas who had to take the empty bottle to the chemist to get some more.

"Hawu!" he said when he saw me. "Why you so dirty?"

I looked down. My right side was smeared with grass and mud and the pocket was torn. "I jumped out of a window."

"Don't be telling fibs."

"I'm not. Edgar jumped too. And now he's at the hospital."

He stared at me. He never knew when I was saying things just to start a game. "Go change into short so I can soak it the dungaree." He loved having things to soak and wash. It gave him a chance to go to the laundry and talk to the other servants.

When he was gone, I settled into the wicker chair. "Dad," I said, "can't you just wake up for once and listen to me?" Tears were running down my cheeks. If Edgar wasn't dead, I was going to have to be paid by Mr. Harding to be his nanny. Ma was going to fly away as soon as she could, and what was the point of a father when he was half dead himself? When I saw other girls' fathers, I couldn't help wanting them half dead as well. All I could think about these days was being dead or half dead, and how I could escape, who would come along to save me.

Phineas came creeping in just as I was wiping my face on the sheet. "Too late to cry," he said. "Big, big trouble!"

"What?"

"Edgar his arm broken, his tongue broken too."

I climbed onto the bed and stretched out along the sheet next to my father.

"No good smiling. Big trouble when Ma she come home."

"You can't break a tongue," I said, sticking mine out at him.

"You pulling tongues, I tell Ma."

"Dad," I said, ignoring Phineas, "Mr. Harding wants me to make Edgar wild and daring, and that's impossible."

Phineas snorted. "You turn Edgar into wild animal maybe."

"Dad," I said, "won't you just wake up for once and tell Mr. Harding to take a running jump at himself?"

"He never move the finger if you rude."

"But, Dad, he keeps telling me what to do as if he's my father, and he isn't! And it's not fair!"

Phineas flapped his hand in front of my face. "Shhh! Look! That finger it move!"

"But what does it mean?" I wailed. "Dad! What's the point of moving your fingers if we don't know what you're trying to say?"

Chapter 7

To make things worse, Bunch came down for the Easter holidays. "Troubles come not single-handed," she said, bashing in with her suitcases. "Golly! What a place!"

"Bunch," Ma said, "kindly keep your comments to yourself."

Bunch cocked her head to one side. "All I said was——"

"I know what you said."

Ma had been complaining ever since she'd received Bunch's postcard. How was she supposed to cope with that creature in this place, she wanted to know? And yet how could she refuse? Who else would take her? Our Jewish Home would let someone like her in only if the family could pay. And we were the family. And so forth.

"Bunch," I said, "did you know this place has ghosts?" She was always seeing curtains moving when there wasn't even a breeze, and reading tea leaves, and then setting off the dogs with her barking scream.

"Ha!" she roared. "You're just trying to fool me!"

"But it has! They come over the wall at night. They may look like natives in the back lane, but really they're ghosts." It was easy to make a joke of things with Bunch, but I badly wanted someone else waking up with me. I wanted anything that would bring Ma down the passage again, switching on the lights and telling me I hadn't even been born during the war.

Bunch frowned. "Does Miranda see them?" She was in Miranda's room now because Miranda had a boyfriend and wouldn't be caught dead letting anyone else kiss her on the lips. Every afternoon Derek waited outside the shop for her, and sometimes, on a Saturday, they went dancing on ice at the rink. Since he'd come along, Miranda was more secretive than ever. "Mind your own beeswax," she'd say to me. "Go and play with Edgar."

"Miranda's got a boyfriend," I said to Bunch.

"In her room?"

Ma swung around. "For God's sake, Bunch, get a grip on yourself!" She slammed the post onto the kist and stormed off to the lounge. But the trouble with storming off in that place was that you couldn't storm very far. So soon she was back, carrying *Shakespeare: The Complete Works* and saying, "I'm going out for a walk."

"Where does she go?" Bunch said.

"To the summerhouse."

"What summerhouse?"

"Mr. Harding's. She meets him down there sometimes."

Bunch cocked her head. "Does your father know about this?"

"I told him, but he doesn't listen."

"Well, he'll certainly listen to me."

Bunch had always prided herself on being able to talk to my father. She would sit in his room, chattering away at him, making up his answers. He was the one who'd given her the nickname in the first place, no one knew why, not even Bunch.

"He wants to know what happened to the dogs," she said at supper. "And he's not at all pleased that you gave up the old house."

Ma huffed at the sideboard. "Fruit salad, Bunch?"

"Also, he'd like his radio. He likes listening to the news."

"Bunch! Would you or would you not like some fruit salad?"

"I would, I would. But really, what happened to his radio?"

Ma handed the bowl to Phineas. "As a matter of fact, I'm going to listen to the radio myself now. If you have any more bright ideas, perhaps you'd like to jot them down and leave them in the bowl on the kist."

Bunch nodded. She knew when she was being scolded. Maybe she knew other things too, it was hard to tell.

"Bunch," I whispered, "did you tell him? What did he say?"

"He's not at all pleased. He's livid, in fact."

"Bunch," I said, cozying up a bit closer, "tell me what he was like before. I mean when he was normal." I was always asking her this, and usually she just told me how he'd brought her special presents when he came home from England, how he'd taken her to the beachfront for candy floss and toffee apples. "Not the beachfront," I said. "I mean what was he like otherwise?"

"He loved cricket, of course. Oh, and marron glacé, tinned asparagus, caviar."

"I know all that. But what else?"

She scrunched her lips up under her nose. "You want me to tell you things I'm not supposed to tell you," she said. "No! I won't! I can't! They'll kill me if I tell."

I sat forward. "What things? What?"

"Just things. Curiosity killed the cat."

"Bunch, I'll give you anything you want. What do you want?"

She pushed out her lips hideously. "Hmm. I want, I want, I want to go to the beach tomorrow."

"I'll take you. I will. We'll go down on the bus."

"I want, I want, I want some candy floss."

"I'll get you some. Now *tell* me."

"Promise you won't tell?"

"Promise! Cross my heart and hope to die."

"That's for Christians."

"Bunch! I promise I'll never cross my heart again!"

She took one of her deep breaths and blew it out all over me. "Welllll——," she said.

I waited, pretending to examine the hem of my dress.

"He was in a fight. With that lot." She jerked her head towards the big house.

"A fight? With who?"

"Whom."

"Bunch! With *whom*!"

"Mr. Charles."

"Who's Mr. Charles?"

"Oh dear, oh dear!" She buried her face in her hands. "I'm going to get it now!"

"You won't, you won't! Who's Mr. Charles?"

She didn't look up. "Harding, of course."

I stared at her hard. "Mr. Harding's brother?"

She nodded.

"What happened? Where?"

"On the golf course-of-course-of-course-of-course!"

"Bunch, I'm not taking you to the beach unless you tell me why they had a fight."

"Don't shout."

"I'm not shouting," I whispered. "Bunch, I'll get you candy floss *and* a toffee apple." I licked at the air. "Because what? *Tell* me!"

She darted a look towards the lounge. Every Saturday night Ma and Miranda sat in there, listening to Lux Radio Theatre, and sometimes I did too. "Because you were in your mother's stomach," she gabbled. "And she was going to run away with Mr. Charles and leave poor old Malcolm and Miranda behind. So they had a fight, and then Mr. Charles ran off to the war because of bashing your father—except, of course, he might not even have been your real father, because everyone knew your mother was going to run off with Mr. Charles——"

Suddenly she clapped her hands over her head and moaned loudly. She sank her head onto the table mat, knocking over the bowl. "Oh! OH! OH NO!" she shouted. "Now I'm going to get it! She's going to blame me! And it's all your fault!"

Chapter 8

For a whole week I stood at the bottom of my father's bed, trying to see him as a stranger. But it was impossible. Even though I knew he might not be my real father, still he belonged to me more than to anyone else—even Miranda, even Bunch.

"For your information," I said to him, "I can get Bunch to tell me anything I like now, so don't think I can't." All week she'd been keeping dead quiet—no blurting out, no frowns or funny looks. "Dad, if Bunch was lying, move a finger."

Nothing.

"And if she's telling the truth?"

Nothing.

I shook the bed hard. "You're a liar!" I shouted. "You're a worse liar than anyone I know!"

"Hawu!" said Phineas, running in. "Why you shout at your father? What the matter with you?"

"He's not my father!" I shouted, turning on him now. "And you knew too! Everyone knew! And no one ever told me!"

He set about putting the tea things back on the tray. "You say bad things, God he punish you."

"Anyway, I'm glad!" I shouted. "Miranda will never be invited to the big house, not in a million years, and neither will Ma."

"Big house it's nothing."

"It's not nothing! It's not nothing!"

But he just pressed his lips closed. He was a minister in the Zionist Church and scared of telling lies. Every Sunday he put on his blue-and-white robes and went down to the river to sing and dance with other servants.

"Keeping it a secret is a lie!" I shouted. "You're a liar whether you like it or not!"

"Don't say bad things," he said. "Here is your father."

"Rubbish!" I screamed. "He's not my father! And you're the liar! You're a terrible liar!"

"Crickey! What's all the shouting about?" Bunch lumped in with her recorder. If Ma wasn't home, she often came in to play for my father. He and Phineas were the only ones who didn't tell her to shut up.

She laid the recorder down on the bedside table and began to straighten the sheet under my father's arms. Then she bent to kiss him on the forehead.

"Don't kiss him!" I shouted. "Your kisses are disgusting! Everyone says so! And he can't even wipe them off!"

"Why you so rude to Auntie now?" said Phineas. "What the matter with you?"

"Get away from him!" I shouted, grabbing the recorder. "GET—AWAY—FROM—MY—FATHER!" I yelled, slamming it hard on the windowsill with every word. I would have slammed her with it, too, except that she'd run for the door, and Phineas had put himself between us.

"OH!" she cried from the doorway. "OH! My RECORDER!"

But Phineas had already snatched it away from me. "Hawu!" he said. "Why you break Miss Bunch her corder?"

"Oh!" Bunch cried, clapping her hands over her head. "Oh! Look!" She turned and turned in the doorway, her whole fat face red and blotched. In our old house, when something bad happened to her, she just lumped off to her room and locked the door. Or she took her recorder and went down to the bottom of the garden and played it there. But here she was forbidden to go into the Hardings' garden or to lock herself into anyone's room, especially Miranda's. Miranda had begun to complain that Bunch snored like a trumpet, and that once, on her way back from the lav in the middle of the night, she'd climbed into Miranda's bed by mistake. "Mistake, my foot!" Ma snorted. And she gave Miranda a Ping-Pong bat to keep under her pillow in case it happened again.

"Bunch," I said, "I'll get you another one."

"You said we'd go to the beach," she sniffed. "You said you'd buy me candy floss."

"I will, I will."

"But I'm leaving tomorrow!" she wailed.

"Look the fingers!" Phineas said. "Master he say no more fighting please, Miss Cress. He say time to be nice to Auntie."

I went to look out into the courtyard. Even Edgar wasn't there today. But if he had been, what difference would it have made? He was a freak just like Bunch, just like everyone at Harding's Rest, my father included. So what was the point of blaming Bunch? What was the point of blaming anyone for what no one on earth could fix?

Chapter 9

Mr. Harding didn't bother to wear his hat anymore when I came to his study. He just tilted his head and said, "Well, Cressida, how are we progressing with Edgar?"

Except for that jump, there was never anything to tell. So I just made things up. "Edgar's keen on going to the beach," or "He wants me to show him how to use a foofy slide."

"What's a foofy slide?"

"A long rope with a wheel on it, and if you hang on to the handle——"

"Yes, yes. What else?"

I stared down at my sandals, pretending to think.

"Well?"

"He wants to know about the war."

"Ah! What is it he wants you to tell him?"

I looked up. You could never tell what Mr. Harding believed. He put down his pipe and sat forward. "Go on, go on."

"He wants to know about the Germans," I mumbled, my own face hot. "I mean, what would have happened if they'd won."

He sat back, twisting his head to stare at me. When I'd told him about Bunch's recorder, he'd stared like this and then he'd pulled out a wad of money and said, "Buy a new one and bring me back the change." And once I'd taken the money, I'd had to take it every month afterwards whether I wanted to or not, because if I tried shaking my head he'd just say, "Don't be tiresome please, Cressida. Here."

"You know about the concentration camps?" he said.

I nodded.

"Then you know what would have happened to you if the Germans had won. Unless, of course, you had been very, very lucky."

"I wouldn't have been lucky."

"No, probably not."

I looked up at him. Even Phineas would have said, "You always lucky! Look how lucky!" Even Ma would say, "You? You'd outwit a fox!"

"In fact," he said, "Edgar might be considered the lucky one, if you can call anything about that unfortunate specimen lucky. But that's another matter."

I could hardly breathe for the hard sound of his voice, his cold eye staring at me.

"Can you fight?" he asked suddenly.

"Fight?"

"With your fists, I mean, like this." He punched into the air as if he were boxing.

I shook my head. I was getting used to his mad questions—Can you sing in tune? Can you tell a silk purse from a sow's ear?—and usually I tried to give a clever answer, something that would make him say, "Ah, there's my Cressida!" But now all I could think of was that somehow Edgar was luckier than I was, and, if it weren't for him, I'd never even have been invited to the big house in the first place.

"Pity," he said, "because Edgar is starting at Somerset after the holidays, and I want him to be able to defend himself."

"As a boarder?" If Edgar went back to boarding school, my money would come to an end. Every week I put it in my biscuit tin and put the tin on top of my wardrobe, where not even Phineas would find it. If he did, he'd tell Ma, and she'd take it right back to the big house like the forks and the serving spoon, because no one was going to turn a child of hers into a servant, not even Mr. Harding.

"As long as he stays here, we're never going to make any headway, I'm afraid." He shook his head and picked up a book from the arm of his chair. "Here. This is one of his set works. Perhaps you'll have better luck with him in the scholarship department."

I bit my lip. I hated failing, even with Edgar. But the last time I'd tried to make him wild, he'd only got to the first branch of the avocado-pear tree before he refused to go any farther or even to come down again. So I'd had to fetch the garden boy, and he'd had to bring a ladder and carry Edgar down over his shoulder like a baby.

"I don't want to do it anymore," I mumbled, placing the book on the elephant's foot.

But he didn't seem to hear. He was filling his pipe with tobacco, lighting it, closing his mouth around it, and then, just as I was getting used to his good side, he turned to blow smoke out through his nostrils. And I knew I'd never get used to the sight of him. Never.

"I don't think I want to come over anymore," I said more boldly.

He nodded, going on with the pipe.

So I stood up. "I have to go now, Mr. Harding," I said. "Thank you very much——"

"Sit down!" he barked, fixing his good eye on me. "We had a bargain, you and I. Have you forgotten?"

"I'll bring the money back."

"Damn the money!"

"But Edgar is hopeless!" I shouted, tears storming down my cheeks now. "He's slower than Miranda, even my mother says so! I don't care if he's lucky! I don't want to come here anymore! And you can't make me! I don't even care if you're my real uncle!"

"What?" he said, looking up. "What was that?"

When I didn't answer, he pulled a handkerchief out of his pocket and held it out to me. "Here," he said, "blow your nose."

But touching his handkerchief would be almost as horrible as touching his nose. I locked my hands behind my back.

"As you please," he said, putting it back. "But it may relieve you to know that my brother went to his death as to a refuge. Which is to say, he had no interest at all in claiming any offspring. Or their mothers, for that matter."

"But I don't *want* him to claim me!" I shouted.

He barked out one of his horrible laughs, making the dogs leap up and run for the door. "You, Cressida, may be one of the few who is lucky enough to be able to choose. Don't you think you should consider yourself lucky after all?"

I shook my head.

"All right, all right. Let me tell you this then: you are your father's child in every way imaginable except for your sex. If your mother hasn't told you this before, I presume she has her reasons."

Mr. Harding never lied, he never needed to. So why did I hate him now for telling me the truth?

"Look," he said, "why don't we just abandon the idea of your toughening up Edgar? It was a Herculean task, I do admit. Will you simply read his set works with him? Agreed?"

He played with the dogs like this, pretending to throw a ball and still keeping it in his hand.

"Cressida, Cressida," he said, leaning forward, "tell me something. When you dream of the future, how do you see yourself in it?"

Suddenly I wondered if I could get him interested in Miranda instead. She'd failed form four again, and Ma was letting her leave school and serve in the shop all day. It wasn't exactly a question of a brain going to waste, Ma said, and, for her own part, she'd like to see out her thirties lying on the couch and listening to *Portia Faces Life,* ha-ha she didn't think!

"Miranda wants to——"

"Bugger Miranda! What is it that you dream of? For yourself?"

I frowned, pretending to think. But even if I could have found the words for an answer, what business was it of his how I used to climb to the top of our old flamboyant and sit up there looking out to sea? Sometimes I'd sing up there, too, at the top of my lungs. And then it was as if everyone in the world knew who I was, and there was nowhere I couldn't go, no one who'd ever be able to stop me.

"I dream of having our house back," I said.

"That's not what I'm after. Try again."

I shrugged. This was worse than playing with Edgar.

"All right, all right, Cressida," he said at last. He reached behind him and brought out a book. "Ever read *Great Expectations*? No? Well, it's about a very lucky fellow. Ha!"

I took the book from him. "Must I still come for tea on Saturday?"

"'Must'? 'Must'?" He laughed. "Ah, Cressida! Yes indeed, you must. Let's say four o'clock? Every Saturday? At the customary rate?"

*

As soon as I came into her room, Ma spied the book. She was almost as jealous of Mr. Harding's books as she was of my going to the big house. "What makes him so sure that we don't have a whole shelf of Dickens ourselves?" she snapped. "Why doesn't he just hire a tutor for that boy? It isn't as if he doesn't have the money."

Usually she was in a good mood on a Saturday, with Film Society to look forward to and dressing up to do. She'd stand at her wardrobe, saying, "What do you think? This one? Or this one?"

But now she just rolled up a stocking and began to pull it on. "What does he expect you to achieve with that half-wit of his? Does he think you'll get him through matric? Ha! That's a tall order!"

"Why is Edgar so lucky?" I asked, sinking into her chair.

"Lucky? What are you talking about?"

"Mr. Harding said so."

She began on the other stocking. "Mr. Harding this, Mr. Harding that—I'm getting a little bit sick of you and Mr. Harding, if you ask me." She turned to check her seams in the mirror.

"But lucky how?"

She gave up and looked straight at me. "That boy grew up in a crèche and never knew his parents. Does that sound lucky to you?"

I stared at her. "Were they burned up in the gas chambers?"

"Gas chambers? What on earth are you talking about?"

I shrugged. If I told her about the books, Phineas would get into trouble. "Mr. Harding was talking about the war."

"Gas chambers!" she hissed. "That boy grew up right here, in Morningside. And anyway, no one was burned up in a gas chamber. They were gassed in gas chambers, and then incinerated afterwards. Ghugh!"

Whatever the case, Edgar could have any fixation he liked and everyone just had to make allowances, whether they liked it or not. Even Fiona McKenzie wasn't as lucky as that. Her parents were dead, too, and she had to live with her grandmother, and wear other people's old school uniforms because her bursary wasn't enough for new ones. And it didn't make any difference how many times Miss Tapscott told us to be kind to her. She was poor and fat and stupid, and no one would let her join in, never mind what anyone said, not even Myfanwy Jones.

"Who were Edgar's parents then?" I asked.

"How would I know?"

"But he's Mr. Harding's nephew."

"In a manner of speaking I suppose he is." She sat down at the dressing table to put on her lipstick.

"Well, I hate teaching him!" I shouted.

She turned around at last. "If you don't want to teach him, just tell Mr. Harding you have better things to do. What on earth is the matter with you?"

I opened *Great Expectations* and pretended to read, but tears began to splash onto the page. Even when I held my breath, still they kept coming.

"Oh, now look!" Ma said, coming to sit next to me on the divan and pulling me close. "Look, darling, why don't I just speak to Mr. Harding tomorrow? I'll tell him you have much too much schoolwork of your own to do. No? Then will you tell him yourself? Good! You just take that book right back where it came from and tell him we have a whole set of Dickens ourselves, and thank you very much anyway. That should put an end to this nasty little arrangement."

Chapter 10

But I didn't tell Mr. Harding. For one thing, I loved *Great Expectations* from the start, and so did Edgar. After I'd been to Mr. Harding's study, we'd go down to the summerhouse, and he would sit on the top step, stripping the fronds off the ferns while I read to him. If things got too frightening or too sad, he'd put his hands over his ears and close his eyes. And when we came to the bits about the Agéd P, he laughed so hard in that high-pitched squeal of his that he wet his trousers, and Mrs. Arbuthnot put all the blame on me.

And then, the next thing, Miranda got herself into trouble with Derek, and Ma forgot all about me. It was just what one might have expected, she shouted, marching up and down, and no, there would certainly *not* be any sort of wedding dress and veil, what was Miranda thinking? She could just take herself down to the magistrate's office in her pink taffeta like every other cheap bit of fluff, and the sooner the better. As to a honeymoon, ha! She should count herself lucky to have the long weekend in the cheap little flat Ma had found for them down on the beachfront.

No one, not even I, could ask Ma who she thought she was, calling Miranda a cheap bit of fluff when she herself had almost run off with Mr. Charles. Miranda was turning her into a laughingstock, Ma said, and if I was planning something to make her life even more ridiculous she'd very much like some warning.

As long as Miranda was getting the blame, I didn't mind Ma's grumbling. I had Miranda's room now, and if I woke up screaming, Ma couldn't help hearing me.

"I don't mind telling you that I blame George Harding for this," she'd say, grumbling in with the DDT. "What business has he, talking to you about the war? Lucky? I'd like to see how lucky he'd feel being woken up night after night by bloodcurdling screams."

There was no point in arguing, and anyway I hardly understood it myself. Every night now, I would lie in bed, thinking of Edgar's mother running naked past German soldiers, his father lying naked in a heap of dead bodies. As long as I was awake it was just a sort of game, and I knew perfectly well it couldn't happen to me. But then, as soon as I was asleep, back came the Germans, and Mr. Harding with them. And the next thing, there was Ma, turning on the lights and blaming it all on him.

"Ma," I said, "why did Mr. Harding give us those concentration-camp books?"

She frowned, and for a moment I thought she'd blame me for finding them, or Phineas for letting me. But she didn't. There was still Film Society to look forward to that night—and a new yellow dress and bolero she'd got Miranda to run up for her. So she just settled onto the couch and told me how Mr.

Harding had been in a concentration camp himself—not as a Jew, of course, but as a prisoner of war—and so he'd seen all sorts of unspeakable things.

And then, one day, he and a few other prisoners had stolen some German uniforms and marched right out of the gate, under the noses of the guards. Most of them were captured and shot, of course, but not Mr. Harding, oh no. He found his way back to his battalion, and then up he went again in his plane, only to be shot down in his ball of fire a few months later.

So there he'd been in hospital, bandaged head to toe, with all the time in the world to brood about the unspeakable things he'd seen. By the time he came home after the war, he was like the Ancient Mariner about it, and she didn't mind saying she blamed him for infecting Miranda with his fixation, too. The girl had always been a sort of creeping Jesus, sneaking in where she wasn't wanted. He hadn't noticed, of course. All he *said* he wanted was for Ma to understand what could have happened to my father if he'd gone off to war himself. And how could she, with her first-class matric and not much else, argue with a man who'd gone to Cambridge? How could she tell him that she happened to know any number of Jews who'd gone off to the war, and come home again, and never ever been anywhere near a gas chamber?

"Dad," I said, settling into the wicker chair, "Ma's talking behind Mr. Harding's back now too. And she's jealous of the big house. And it only makes it worse every time I have to go over."

It was true. Every week there was something new. Either she'd be sending me over with a plate of Phineas's butter biscuits, or she'd be wanting to know why no one had even bothered to thank her for them. And then, one Saturday, while I was having tea as usual on the verandah, there she came herself, sailing across the lawn with her book and sunhat, down to the summerhouse to read.

"Ah, there goes your mother again," Mrs. Arbuthnot said. "One of these days, no doubt, she'll be bringing a banjo to serenade us."

If Mr. Harding were there, she'd never have dared to say a thing like that. But he hardly ever came out to tea; he had a tray sent to his study. And when he was ready to see me, he rang the bell, and the houseboy would come to call me, and Mrs. Arbuthnot would say, "Kindly remember your manners this time, Cressida."

"And that cow Mrs. Arbuthnot is jealous, too," I said. "And I don't see why I've got to put up with it."

"Hawu," said Phineas. He was fussing with the pills, counting them out into a little glass bowl. "That one housekeeper she make big trouble everywhere."

"See?" I said to my father. "See? She's even horrible to old Mrs. Harding! And I'm going to tell Mr. Harding. I'm the only one he ever listens to anyway."

That was true, too. When I'd asked him if it was possible to cut down the wild bananas because mosquitoes were tormenting my father, he wanted to know why no one had mentioned it before. And then, the next thing, the wild bananas were gone, and there was the man from the mosquito department again, and Ma inviting him in for a cup of tea herself this time.

"And I don't think old Mrs. Harding's all that mad either," I said. "I think she puts it on a lot."

"Ê-hê!" said Phineas, settling in with his history set work. History was one of his subjects for night school, and when I came home from school now he was full of questions.

"What this mean, *subsistence*?" "Where this funny place, *Addis Ababa*?" If I didn't know, I never admitted it. I just showed him how to look things up for himself in the dictionary or the *Children's Encyclopedia*. So there he sat now in my father's room, reading the dictionary. "This one writing too tiny," he'd say, squinting at the page. "Soon I'm asking the Madam for the glasses."

But if Ma found out he was reading the dictionary, she'd blame me when he got a job as a driver. And then she'd just fly away, and I'd be the one left counting out the pills and coping with Bunch when she came down for the holidays. "I'll buy you the glasses," I said.

*

"Well, what's the subject of discussion for today?" said Mr. Harding. He always asked this, and usually we would come quickly around to the war. There were things I should know, he said, not only about the Germans, but also about the Poles and the Russians, the Spanish, the French—all the people over all the centuries who had blamed the Jews for their own misfortunes.

And so, after a while, it began to feel as if Mr. Harding was the only one who understood that it didn't matter if you hadn't been born during the war, you could still want to know what had happened in it. When I asked if it was true that the Germans pulled out fingernails with pliers and threw babies into the air so they could shoot them like pigeons, he just closed his eyes and shook his head and said, "Worse than that, my dear. Much worse than that. What they didn't murder they warped, even a generation beyond. Just look at me—not the face, not the head, those are the legitimate wages of war—but the rest of it, everything I've been left with, down to the dreadful sense of

having colluded with evil simply by having survived the sight of
it. Does that make any sense to you? Does it?"

I nodded, although evil was one thing and Germans coming through the window quite another. Still, if I tried to ask
what he had actually seen himself, like the things I'd read in
the books, he'd just close his eyes and shake his head and say,
"One day perhaps I'll write a book about it." And then, the
next thing, we'd be on to an opera or what Garibaldi had accomplished in Italy, good and bad.

*

"Is our old house empty again?" I asked. I'd walked down the
hill after school just to have a look. The people who'd bought
it had fallen on hard times, Ma told me, and were going to
have to sell, which served them right, coming in with all their
airs and graces. I'd looked in through the gate. The curtains
were gone, and there was a cement mixer next to the front
steps, ladders on the verandah.

"It is and it isn't," he said. "Why?"

I blushed. You could never hide things from Mr. Harding.
Even though he only had one good eye, he had a way of keeping it on you until you came out with the truth.

"Ah, Cressida, Cressida!" he said, pushing himself up and
walking over to the wooden box he kept on the table. He often gave me things from that box—a lion's tooth, a small ivory
elephant. "Here," he said, holding out an old, cracked papier-
mâché mask. "Put this on and go and have a look at yourself
in the mirror."

It was a doll's face, with eyelashes and rouge and a beauty
spot under one eye. I held it by its stick and stared at it.

"Go on, go on," he said. "Take it over and look." He
loved testing me like this, but usually it was with a book or a

record. He'd have one ready when I came in, and then either he'd read from the book or play the record, and if I didn't know what it was, he told me to take a flying guess. And if I still didn't know, he sent me home with it so I could give him a proper answer next time.

I walked over to the mirror and held the mask up to my face. It smelled of old dust and stale perfume, and I tried not to let it touch my skin.

"Well?" he said. "What do you see?"

"A lady."

"Wrong!"

"A doll?"

He sighed. "What you see, my dear, is a woman, just a woman. A woman of the night, if you will. A courtesan. A trollop. A tart." He gave out one of his roaring laughs. "Can you work out why I wanted you to try it on?" He was over at the gramophone now, putting on a record. Perhaps he'd want me to sing, you could never tell with him. When he found out that we'd had to sell our old piano, he said I should come and practice on the big-house instrument. It needed exercise, he said, and there was no hope that Edgar would ever do much more than play chopsticks, if that. Often he seemed to forget he'd asked me to come over for Edgar in the first place. So there I was every afternoon, and there was old Mrs. Harding in the rocking chair, barking "Count, girl! Count!"

"Is Mozart not the most glorious of all, Cressida?"

I nodded. Somehow I could never admit to him how much I loved the music he played for me. It would have been like telling him about my dream of the future—he'd have taken it for himself. And then it would never be the same again.

"*Madamina*," he sang out in the deep, echoing voice that always embarrassed me. "*Il catalogo è questo delle belle che amò il padron mio.* Come over here, Cressida, and see if you can work this out."

On the table he had opened the big leather photo album to a page with snaps of a soldier—smoking a cigarette; standing next to a plane, smiling; lined up in a row with other soldiers, their arms around each other. "Well?"

"They're you," I said.

"Of course, of course they are! But what else?"

I shrugged. He was always telling me to be frank, but how could I tell him that it didn't matter how many pictures he showed me of himself, I'd never be able to see him as a normal person, never?

He took the needle off the record and went to the mirror, turning to look at his bad side. "What you see here, Cressida —this monster, this vision of Hell—this, Cressida, is the man who was hiding behind that cocky young chap in the photographs. Does it make any sense now?"

I nodded. If Germans could come climbing over walls even though I knew the war was over, why shouldn't Mr. Harding always have been a monster, or my father just sit up in bed one day and say, "Hello, where have you been hiding?"

"The point is," he said, "you cannot have your house back the way it was because *you* are not the same. In fact, you are becoming more yourself every time I see you."

I longed to know what he meant, but if I asked he'd only give me another test. So all I said was, "A house isn't a person."

He cocked his head to look at me properly. He liked it when I argued. "How so?"

"Because it's still there. It's still the way it was."

"True, true. The analogy is not entirely sound and I am certainly practicing a little sophistry on you. But the advice remains the same: remember your house the way it was when you were the way you thought you were in it."

"Who has it now?"

"An extremely vulgar racing-car driver. English, I'm afraid. He's putting in a swimming bath and a gaming room and God knows what else. If you'd like a cure for your nostalgia, I'll arrange for you to see it when he's accomplished his transformations."

*

"Dad," I said, "sometimes Mr. Harding's not as much of a freak as Bunch."

"Hawu," said Phineas, looking up from the *Children's Encyclopedia*. "Why you rude about Auntie?"

"Someone's bought our house again," I said. "And he's putting in a proper swimming bath. Mr. Harding's going to take me to see."

"Why he want to do that?" Phineas was almost as curious about what went on with Mr. Harding as Ma was. He had strict ideas about children, and was strict with his own children, too, much stricter than he was with me. When they came down from Zululand to visit him, I'd hear him shouting at them, hitting them, and then crying—pitiful crying. "They cheek their mother," he'd say. "They got to learn." But when I asked Ma why they couldn't all just come and live in the big-house servants' quarters now that there was room, she suggested that perhaps I should consider taking over the running of the country myself. It couldn't possibly be a madder place than it was already, she said, and it would keep me out of her hair.

Chapter 11

And then one Saturday everything began to change. It all started when old Mrs. Harding's false teeth came loose and landed in her teacup, and, for once, Edgar burst into a high-pitched squealing laugh.

"Edgar!" Mrs. Arbuthnot cried. "You are excused from the table!"

"May I be excused too?" I said, standing up.

"You sit down!" she barked at me, banging on the table so that the tea things jumped.

"Stupid old cow!" lisped old Mrs. Harding. She was always calling Mrs. Arbuthnot a stupid old cow, and usually Mrs. Arbuthnot pretended not to notice. But this time Edgar was still squealing in the doorway, and old Mrs. Harding was pushing herself up from the table, saying, "*I* don't have to excuse myself in my own house, do I?"

"Mrs. Harding," I said quickly. "My mother said she'll take you for a drive along the beachfront if you like."

"Your mother *what*?" snapped Mrs. Arbuthnot. "Edgar! Mrs. Harding! Will everyone kindly come back to the tea table at once!"

"Get stuffed!" lisped old Mrs. Harding, beginning to move off. "I'm going to find Charles. I want him to know what's going on out here."

Mrs. Arbuthnot jumped up herself then and grasped old Mrs. Harding by the arm. "You haven't even finished your cake," she said.

But old Mrs. Harding hated being touched by Mrs. Arbuthnot. She would make a show of brushing at the spot with her hand or clattering her false teeth like a baboon. This time she swung her handbag around in a circle, hitting Mrs. Arbuthnot on the side of her head.

"Aii!" Mrs. Arbuthnot screamed. "BITCH!" she shouted.

"Serves you right!" said old Mrs. Harding quite calmly. "Now what have you done with my teeth?"

"I'll get them." I jumped up and ran around the table to fish them out of the teacup.

There was another squeal from Edgar when he saw them dripping between my fingers. They were still warm, and had silver wires around the back, and if they weren't old Mrs. Harding's I'd have thrown them away like a spider.

"Thank you, my dear," she said, slipping them into place. "Now why don't we go and tell Charles all about it."

"I'll tell him!" Mrs. Arbuthnot shrieked. "Mark my words! He'll hear about this from me!"

"Hear about what?" said Mr. Harding. He was standing in the doorway with his hand on Edgar's shoulder.

"Charles!" said old Mrs. Harding. "What on earth are you wearing on your head?"

"I've had enough!" shrieked Mrs. Arbuthnot. "I've reached my limit! She knows perfectly well you're George, not Charles! She's just doing it to provoke me!"

"Mrs. Arbuthnot!" said Mr. Harding, "would you kindly *stop* that noise?"

"I can't take her anymore!" Mrs. Arbuthnot shrieked on. "It's not as if I haven't tried! It's not as if——"

"Mrs. Arbuthnot!" he barked. "If you do not quieten down, I shall have to ask you to remove yourself." Mr. Harding hated the sound of women shrieking Phineas had told me. Whenever a fight started up between the laundry girl and the cook, out he would come with his head on fire and his riding crop at the ready.

"P.S., wasn't someone supposed to take me for a drive along the beachfront?" said old Mrs. Harding.

"Cressida," Mr. Harding said, "you and Edgar are to take yourselves off for an hour or so. I don't want to see you back here until five o'clock."

*

"How old were you when your father died?" I asked Edgar. We were sitting on the verandah of my old house, looking out over the garden.

"What if they catch us?" he whispered. "What if they tell Uncle?"

"Maybe he's not even your real uncle," I said.

"Rot."

"Have you ever seen pictures of your parents?"

He shook his head.

"Do you think I look like my father? I mean, if he were normal. Look!" I poked him.

He frowned, forcing himself to look up at me. Usually he hated looking at people, any people, and so I'd got used to talking to his ear or his forehead or to the back of his head. "Can we go back now?" he said.

I stretched out along the verandah floor. The pillars were so overgrown with golden shower that he was just a dark shape against them. "Talking to you is like talking to no one," I said. "If I look at you I see nothing."

But it was impossible to insult Edgar. He would just stay where he was until someone told him not to.

I jumped up and kicked off my sandals. "I'm going to go inside," I said, running off around the verandah to try the doors and windows. "All locked," I said, coming around again. I ran down into the garden and along the path, around to the side, with Edgar creeping behind me. "That's where our swimming bath used to be," I said, staring down into the deep pit of red earth. And we had a monkeypod tree over there, too."

"Let's go," he said. "Before they find us."

I glanced back up at the verandah. Except for the garden and the golden shower, nothing about the house had changed. The roof was still green, the flamboyant full of flowers. I ran up to it and pulled myself onto the first branch, dancing along to the edge of it and then jumping to make it sway. "Look!" I said. "It's a swing!" I danced back to the trunk and climbed up quickly, right to the top. "See?" I shouted down. "Look!" I crouched on the big top branch and swung out in one leap onto the edge of the roof. "See?" I shouted again, looking down over the gutter.

"Don't jump!" he said, looking up. "Don't, Cressida!"

I crawled along the corrugated iron to the small storeroom window. It was open, and I edged it up and climbed in. The storeroom was just as we'd left it. It smelled of old books and hot dust and varnished teak. Even the Chinese kist was still in the corner. Inside was Ma's old hat and veil, and her long white gloves with the burn mark on one finger. When I'd asked her why we'd had to leave the new people so many of our things, she'd just said she was glad to see the back of them, they'd haunted the best years of her life.

"Cressida?"

I climbed quickly down the steep steps to the kitchen, and then ran through to the front door and opened it. Spitting bugs were still singing in the jacarandas, and the hedge was overgrown. Everything could have been normal, except it wasn't. "Edgar!" I shouted. "Come around to the front!"

"Where did you get the gloves?" he asked when I opened the front door.

I laughed and waved my arms. "Come in!" I said, running in again and through to the dining room. "Oh look!" I stopped dead. Tins of paint were lined up along the wall, with paintbrushes laid out neatly on newspaper. "PAINT! PAINT! PAINT!" I sang out, listening to the word boom and echo around the empty room. "EDGAR! EDGAR! EDGAR!"

He shrank back against the wall. "We're going to get it for coming inside."

"Fraidy cat! Fraidy cat!" I picked up a screwdriver and pried the lid off one tin. "Oh, look!" I said, stirring it up with the screwdriver. "Red! Let's play naughts and crosses!" I dipped a paintbrush and painted a crisscross on the wall. "Here," I said, holding out the brush to him. "You go first."

But he shook his head. "She'll strap me if I get paint on my clothes."

"Who? Mrs. Arbuthnot?"

He nodded.

"Then take them off, I don't care! Look, I'll take mine off too." I pulled off the gloves, and then my blouse and my shorts. "You can keep your underpants on if you like."

"But they'll get paint on them."

"Then take them off, I've seen my father millions of times!" I turned back to the wall and wrote CRESSIDA and EDGAR.

"Don't paint my name," he whispered. He was standing behind me, trying to hide himself with his hands.

"I can see your thing! I can see your thing!" I shouted, flicking my brush at him. "Measles! Measles! You've got measles on your THING!"

Suddenly he grinned, making a grab for the brush.

"Here," I said. "I'll get another one."

And so we began to chase each other around the room, stopping only to dip our brushes into the paint. "Ugly! Ugly!" I shouted, flinging paint at him and then racing off, with him squealing behind me. "Let's paint the way with arrows! Let's paint all the way to the kitchen!"

There was nothing to stop us now, not even a clock. So we painted arrows, and then anything we liked. And, when the paint was almost gone, I tipped the last tin onto the floor, and splashed my feet in it, and made footprints all down the passage to my bedroom, with Edgar following after like a dog.

But when I got to the door, I stopped. The room was nothing now—naked, empty. It was just a small room with my curtains piled in a heap under the basin. Even the window looked naked without the monkeypod tree outside. "It used to be lovely," I said, although I knew he'd never believe me. I didn't believe myself either.

I turned and ran along the passage, past my father's room,

past his bathroom and the linen closet, and through the glass doors to the study.

"Wait for me! Wait!" Edgar shouted. "Wait for me!"

I ran as fast as I could, swinging around the corners. He began to cry behind me, but I didn't care. I knew I'd be blamed for everything, for what he did as well, and really I didn't care. All I wanted was to find more tins of paint, a hammer, anything at all before it was too late. And just as I was thinking that Mr. Harding was the one to blame himself because who had made us move out in the first place, who had told Edgar and me to go anywhere we liked?—just then, there he was at the front door, flicking his riding crop against his boots.

Chapter 12

"Dad," I said, "one of these days I'm just going to run away."

"Where you run to?" said Phineas. He was the only one who didn't keep thinking up new ways to make me sorry for what I'd done. Mr. Harding had made me write a letter to Mr. Ledson, the new owner, and put all the money I'd saved in the envelope with it. And then, when Ma found out about the money, she said I was a Delilah, I was a Jezebel, heartless and grasping, and if I knew what was good for me I'd stay out of her sight until she could bear to have me in it again.

For a whole week I had supper in the kitchen with Phineas. And even that wasn't enough because, when Mr. Ledson went to the house to inspect the damage, I had to go down the road with Ma to say sorry face-to-face. So there I was in the dining room again, and there she was, looking around at the naughts and crosses, and the footprints, and the arrows. And there was

Mr. Ledson shouting, "*Sorry? Sorry?* Is 'sorry' supposed to be enough for all of *this*?"

He was short and ugly, with small pink eyes and a huge, red, swollen, pitted nose. The skin on his face was pitted too, but it was white in an English sort of way, with red veins and thick, pale, freckled lips.

"We shall, of course, compensate you for your costs," Ma said.

"'Compensate'? 'Compensate'?" he shouted on. "A fancy word, madam! But what does it mean? I don't mind telling you that if it weren't for that protector of yours, I'd have turned the lot of you over to the police!"

This was not at all what Ma had expected. All the way down the hill she'd been warning me not even to think of talking back, not to try excusing myself either. I was just to stand there and take my medicine, and she hoped sincerely that it would be good and bitter.

"If *I* had such a child, madam," he said, "I would certainly know what to do! The strap wouldn't be good enough, that I can tell you!"

Until now, with everyone blaming me, it had been easy not to be sorry for what I had done. But suddenly, there was Ma being shouted at when it wasn't even her fault. And she'd put on her yellow dress and bolero, and the pearl earrings my father had given her as an engagement present. With her standing next to me, it seemed impossible that I'd come down the road in the first place, and jumped onto the roof, and never, not once, considered the consequences of anything, not even of this.

"I thought only savages allowed their children to go around wrecking havoc like this," Mr. Ledson shouted. "Or are you one of those modern types? No better than savages yourselves, if you ask me."

I glanced up at Ma. Now was the time for her to tell him that I was a Bad Seed, that I was a Delilah and a Jezebel and she was at her wits' end as to how to cope. But she didn't. She just crossed her arms and glanced around the room as if red paint on the walls and floors was nothing so terrible.

"Perhaps, Mr. Ledson," she said at last, "you might consider what the child has had to contend with, one way and another—forced out of her own house and moved, under straitened circumstances, to something not much bigger than the servants' quarters out there." She paused for a moment to give him time to consider. "As to 'the strap,' as you put it," she said, "I wouldn't dream of resorting to anything as common as that."

"*Common?*" he shrieked. "I'll tell you what's common, madam," he shouted, flinging his arms around the room. "*This* is common! And I'll tell you what else: I have never, not in all my years, seen a girl more in need of the strap than that one standing there! As far as I'm concerned, servants' quarters is too good for the likes of you!"

Ma closed her lips and stared at him the way she stared at Moosah when he was asking too much for his flowers. After a while, if he didn't come down in price, she'd just stalk off to the next stall, and it didn't matter how far Moosah followed her, crying that his wife was sick and his children needed schoolbooks. Nothing mattered once Ma had decided she'd had enough.

"For your information," she said, "it is *wreaking* havoc, not *wrecking* havoc. And servants' quarters are plural. Really, Mr. Ledson, one wonders who the savage is around here."

Mr. Ledson took a few steps towards her. He was snorting

heavily now through that awful nose, staring from one of us to the other with his small, pink eyes. "I've got a good mind to call in the police after all," he said.

And still Ma didn't answer. She just turned to me and said, "Come along, Cressida. I think I've heard quite enough from this common little man for one day."

"*Enough?*" he shouted after us as we made our way down the verandah steps and around to the front of the house. "I'll tell you who's had enough! *I've* had enough! *I'm* the one who's had enough of the likes of *you!*"

But she didn't turn around, and by the time we were in the courtyard, I was crying hopelessly. "Sorry, Ma!" I sobbed, throwing my arms around her. "I'm sorry!"

She didn't push me away, she didn't even seem to remember now that it was all my fault. "Dreadful, vulgar little man!" she said, throwing down her bag on the hall table. "Imagine painting the dining room betel red! Next thing, no doubt, he'll have lace curtains up, and the Venus de Milo in the hall. Ha!" She was looking at her watch, not wanting to be late for Film Society. I knew she'd be really cross by the time she came back. She was always cross after Film Society because everyone else could go trooping off to the Matador to discuss the film over a mixed grill, and she had to come home to a supper of cauliflower cheese and a child bent on ruining what was left of her life.

She jammed a cigarette into the holder. "Whose idea was it that you and that Edgar career around that house in the altogether? Yours, I suppose?"

I shrugged. If she hadn't been starting the bad mood already, I'd have pointed out that Miranda and I had always run around in the altogether when Bunch wasn't down, that all of us did, including her, unless Phineas was there.

"Playing Delilah with a boy too slow to know any better," she grumbled, digging for her lighter.

"But Mrs. Arbuthnot would have strapped him if he had got paint on his clothes," I said.

"What?" She looked up at last. She was always interested in Mrs. Arbuthnot, anything I could tell her.

"She straps him for any little thing," I said. "And also she told him that the stork brought him."

She snorted. People who told their children about storks and Father Christmas and fairies at the bottom of the garden were ignorant and common, she liked to say. How was a child to be prepared for the real world? How to know opportunity from danger when it came knocking at the door with its imploring ways?

"Close the door, please, Cressida," she said, closing her eyes in a cloud of smoke. "And sit down, please. There are a few things you need to know before you get any older."

Part Two

Chapter 13

It was all my fault that Ma married Mr. Ledson. If I hadn't painted the dining room walls, she'd never have been able to lecture him about civilised people, and he'd never have joined the Film Society, which is where it all started. First he offered her a lift home in his sports car, and then, the next week, he trooped her off to the Matador for supper with everyone else. And after that he began calling her his "Queenie" and even named his speedboat "Queenie," too. When I pointed out that "Queenie" was a name people gave their dogs, he just told me to keep my trap shut or he'd shut it for me. And so there was warfare between us from the start.

"Dad," I said, "I wish *you* could just bash *him* over the head with a golf club."

Phineas laughed. I was fifteen now, and he could stop pretending to disapprove of everything I said. Anyway, he was terrified of Mr. Ledson himself. He'd seen the danger long before I did, and went down to Indian town on his day off to buy special oils and herbs with his own money. He grated them and boiled them on the stove, and rubbed the potion into the soles of my father's feet.

But it didn't work. One day, when I came home from school, Phineas was on his knees, wailing. "The Lord Jesus He take the Master for Himself! What it happens to me now? What it happens to my childrens?"

Phineas was prone to hysterics these days. When my father caught a cold and had to be propped up to breathe, he'd moved his mat into my father's room and refused to go back to the servants' quarters except to wash. "Phin," I said, "don't worry. Jesus couldn't have taken him, we're Jewish. Want me to call Ma? Dr. Slatkin?"

I walked over to the bed and bent to listen to my father's breathing. But it was hopeless, I could never tell the difference. "Phin," I said. "Where's Ma?"

He flapped his hand in the direction of our old house. She was always down there now, even when Mr. Ledson wasn't home. He'd given her carte blanche to tell the Indian gardener where to plant what and to choose new curtains, whatever she wanted. Mr. Ledson was far too busy racing his cars and speedboats to concern himself with lounge curtains and beds of seedlings, she said.

"You're going to have to fetch her, Phin," I said. I knew he couldn't stand going down there, but neither could I. "Go on."

He shook his head like a madman. When Ma had told him to go down to the old house and learn a thing or two from Mr. Ledson's cook, he'd just pretended not to remember. "Hawu," he said to me later. "Why I want to go to that old kitchen? What that cook she can teach *me*?"

"All right," I said. "I'll go." But I walked across the driveway instead and into the big house through the kitchen door.

"Hello?" said old Mrs. Harding, poking her head out of the pantry. Wednesday was Mrs. Arbuthnot's day off, and old Mrs. Harding was always on the loose. Sometimes I'd find her milling around our courtyard and then I'd ask her in. "You still lying there, you old fraud?" she'd say to my father, settling into the wicker chair next to his bed. "Anyone going to bring us some tea and jam tarts?"

I ran across the hall and knocked on the study door. "Mr. Harding? Mr. Harding, it's Cressida."

"Yes?" he said. "Come in! What is it, Cressida?" He never liked being disturbed, not even by me.

"Phineas thinks my father has died," I said. "And I'm not sure how to tell."

He jumped to his feet. "Where is your mother?" But he didn't wait for an answer, he just strode through the house without his hat, and out across the driveway, into our courtyard. In all the years we'd been staying there, he'd never once come over, not even when Ma invited him in for a drink. But now there he was, nearly knocking over Phineas as he stormed through the front door.

"Master!" Phineas cried, dropping to his knees again and clutching at Mr. Harding's trousers. "Master! What's it happen to me now? What's it happen to my childrens?"

"What?" Mr. Harding wrenched his leg away. "WHAT?" he roared down at Phineas. "What's going to happen to YOU? I'll tell you what's going to happen to you! I shall personally whip you to within an inch of your miserable life if you don't get up immediately and go and fetch your madam!" He gave Phineas a shove with his boot, sending him scrambling along the floor. And then he walked into my father's room, telling me to wait in the hall outside.

Chapter 14

Mr. Ledson's first wedding had been a rushed affair, Ma said, because he'd been going off to war. And then, when he'd got back, he'd found that his bride had been blown to pieces during the Blitz, her head in one place, a foot somewhere else. So who could blame him for wanting a proper wedding this time, a proper bride?

"It isn't fair," Miranda whispered to me as we stood at the buffet table. "Why is *she* allowed to wear a wedding dress and a veil, and I had to wear my old pink taffeta?"

I nodded, but nothing was fair when it came to Ma and Mr. Ledson. There was really no reason, they said, not to get married a fortnight after my father's funeral, and if anyone thought otherwise, Mr. Ledson himself wanted to hear about it. All these years, his Queenie had been mourning a living death, and who would deny her a little happiness now? Who would deny him either?

There was no answering any of this. It was as if nothing we

had been before would ever matter again, as if Ma herself had never called Mr. Ledson a dreadful, vulgar little man. He was a breath of fresh air, she said now, and unlike some she could name, had had to make his own way, make a go of his racing, and was that not thrilling? Was that not admirable?

Everything about Mr. Ledson was admirable now. So when I tried to remind her that he'd painted the dining room betel red or that all his furniture came in suites from Barron's, she just asked who I thought I was, Lady Muck on Toast? And, what's more, I was kindly to refrain from mentioning anything to do with paint or betel red again or she wouldn't hold herself responsible for the consequences.

There were any number of things I was kindly to refrain from mentioning now, especially Jews. As a Christian, Mr. Ledson had certain ideas about us, Ma said, which, in the fullness of time, she herself would set about altering. But in the meanwhile, would I keep those bloody concentration-camp books out of his sight? Or, better still, would I kindly return them to Mr. Harding?

"Ah," said Mr. Harding, coming up behind me. "So you're back home after all, Cressida?"

I stared down at my plate. "The funeral baked meats," I murmured. All day I had been waiting to utter the line to him, even though I wasn't sure he wouldn't scold me for it.

He helped himself to one of the canapés that Phineas had been making all week. This wedding was Phineas's last hurrah in the kitchen, Ma said. Next week Mr. Ledson was sending him to driving school, and after that he'd be driving her wherever she wanted to go. She was going to take a few courses up at varsity, for instance, which was where she would have been in the first place if she'd had her wits about her. Well, she'd done her penance for that little bit of folly, thank you very much, and now she was putting the past behind her, looking forward to making up for lost time.

Everything, she said, was falling into place now. Miranda had her little house, and her little brood of shopkeepers in the making. Out of the goodness of his heart, Mr. Ledson had taken over the loan on the Cotton Reel, and even Bunch was safely stowed at Our Jewish Home, thanks to him. So that left only me, and I'd either learn to civilise my tongue or she wouldn't hold herself responsible for the consequences there either.

"Harding!" Mr. Ledson came up and clapped him on the shoulder. "Got you to thank for all this, old boy!"

"How so?"

"Well, if you hadn't kept them up there, this little savage wouldn't of come down the hill and did what she did, would she? Then how would I have met my Muriel?"

I could tell by the dip of the veil that Mr. Harding was twisting his face into one of his brutal smiles. It was the way he summoned patience when I gave him a stupid answer, or told him a lie about why I couldn't come the following Saturday. "Botany expedition?" he would say, twisting up. "On a Saturday? Well, get along then! Dismissed!"

Suddenly he put his arm around my shoulders and drew me close. "I'm hoping Cressida won't forsake us," he said. "I've come to count on her, you know."

I looked away. All I could think of now were the things I'd never have again, had never wanted in the first place, although I'd give anything to have them back, even if they came with Germans climbing the wall. I didn't want to choose the furniture and curtains for my old room, I didn't want anything to do with our old house. Mr. Harding was right, I wasn't the same anymore. Nothing was the same, and I'd never be the same again either.

Chapter 15

It didn't matter how much Ma threatened me, I would never call Mr. Ledson "Uncle Albert." If I wasn't allowed to call him Mr. Ledson I'd just call him nothing. And so, from the start, he was nothing to me, and there was nothing his Queenie could do about it.

Every morning she put on one of her new outfits and had Phineas drive her to the university in the new Rover. And then, when I came home from school, there she'd be, stretched out on the swing seat with D. H. Lawrence. She'd started her new life with two courses in English, and everything she read made her look at her old life differently, she said. She never explained what she meant, and I refused to ask. But I put the framed picture of my father next to my bed, and stuck photographs of him all around the walls of my room.

When she saw them there, she stood in the middle of the room with her hands on her hips, her eyes wild, and the silver snake bangle Mr. Ledson had given her biting into her arm. Where did I imagine my future would lie if I refused to put the past behind me, she demanded? And what did I think I was achieving by treating Uncle Albert like a leper? Who did I think was feeding me? Clothing me? How did I imagine I was ever going to be able to go to varsity without Uncle Albert's help?

I didn't bother to answer. Between us now there was a sort of warfare, with her asking questions and me staring back in silence. I'd found the photo albums hidden away in the old Chinese chest, and carried them down to my room. But all I could see when I opened them was the past, with everyone in it except me. So I pulled out the photos I wanted, and if Ma or Miranda were in them, I cut them out with scissors.

"Dad," I said to his photograph, "if you hadn't died, we wouldn't have had to come back here, and I wouldn't have to put up with Mr. Ledson *every single day.*"

Ruth Frank was the only one I could talk to about any of this. One day, walking home from choir practice, she'd asked if I'd like to come up to her house for tea. We'd sat on her verandah, laughing at the other girls in the class, and at Edwina Sloane, whose father had changed his name from Slomovitz because he couldn't bear to be Jewish.

After that it was easy to laugh about anyone, even Mr. Ledson. I told her about his gaming room under the house, and the ankle bracelet he'd given Ma, the look on her face when he tucked his serviette into his collar or pushed his peas onto his fork with his fingers. "Ag!" Ruth said. "Shame! Poor you!"

But as soon as I closed her gate and had to walk back down the hill, nothing was funny anymore. I was the one stuck with Ma and Mr. Ledson, and there were years of it to go, a whole lifetime it seemed before I'd be free of them. And even then what would I do? Who could I ask to help me?

Mr. Harding was out of the question. I'd stopped taking his money when Edgar left for Somerset, and to start again now would be worse than it had been at the start. "Am I seeing the beginnings of pride in my little protégée?" he'd said, twisting into a smile. "If so, I'd suggest you reread Proverbs 16. They must be acquainting you with the Old as well as the New Testaments in Scripture, no?"

But, whatever he said, I wouldn't take it, and after that it was as if I could say no to anything I didn't like, even Sir Walter Scott, and the Ravel pavane he wanted me to learn. If I came up with good reasons, so much the better. He'd just laugh and say, "Ah Cressida, you're coming along rather nicely now, aren't you?"

And then one day, without warning, he wasn't there. He'd gone away on a ship, Phineas said, and wasn't coming back for another three months. When I told Ma, she just laughed. Perhaps he'd come back with a bride at last, she said, and wouldn't that be a boon for everyone, especially poor old Mrs. Harding? He'd be able to get rid of that ghastly Arbuthnot woman, not to mention the mistress he'd been keeping up the coast.

"Mistress?" I rolled my eyes. "What mistress?"

"Oh, you'd be surprised," said Ma, giving me one of her maddening smiles. "He's a man after all, and a very rich one. You may be clever, but there's a great deal of the world you know nothing about."

I slammed off to my room. "Dad," I said, "I can't take much more of it. Maybe I should just run away."

"Hawu!" said Phineas, coming in with my school shoes. "You talking to no one."

"I don't talk to no one!" I shouted. "And kindly knock before you come creeping in here."

He closed his lips and frowned. Now that Mr. Ledson was the one taking care of him, he didn't want to be reminded of my father. Except for polishing the shoes, he hardly ever came into the house anymore. He spent most of his time in the garage, cleaning the cars and talking to the other servants walking past. "Hawu, Miss Cress," he said if I came grumbling to him there. "The Lord He say we must count our blessing."

So usually, I stayed in my room until the bell rang for supper. Ma had had the walls painted yellow and the woodwork white, and she'd chosen the material for new curtains, with a pelmet and bedspreads to match. She'd made me choose prints to hang on the walls and a desk set from Cottam's, and when I told her I hated the room anyway, that it would never be the same again, she just said that the serpent's tooth had lost its bite for her, I might as well try sinking it into someone else.

When she came into the shops now, she didn't even have to ask the salesladies to bring things out from the back. It was "Mrs. Ledson this" and "Mrs. Ledson that," and when we were back in the car she'd say, "If those creatures think I've forgotten how they treated me when I had the world on my shoulders, they'd be quite mistaken."

*

"Ma," I said one day as we were driving home from town, "do you know when Mr. Harding's coming back?"

"Mr. Harding is no longer my concern."

"But he used to be."

"Of course he used to be. He *had* to be. How else were we going to live?"

But I was sick of the way she kept switching and changing everything to suit herself. "So why did you used to meet him down at the summerhouse?"

"Why did I *what*?" She stared at me hard. With Phineas driving we could never fight properly in the car.

"You used to meet him down at the summerhouse," I said, glancing casually out of the window. "I used to see you there. I used to hear what you said as well."

She dropped her voice. "You heard what?"

I didn't answer. We were already climbing the hill, up and up, turning into the garage, and for once I was glad to see Mr. Ledson's car there. Ma never knew when he was coming home. Sometimes he'd be gone for days or even weeks, and then he'd be back suddenly, holding his hands behind his back to make her guess which one had the present in it.

She grasped me by the arm as soon as we were out of the car. But before she could say a word, there he was, calling, "Queenie? Is that you, Queenie?"

She flung my arm away and stiffened into a smile. Whatever she said, I knew Mr. Ledson would always be a common, ignorant little man to her, although she'd go to the ends of the earth before admitting it, and even then she'd find a way to lay the blame on me.

Chapter 16

And then, one day, Phineas came knocking on my door to say that Master Edgar was waiting outside the garage and, no, he wouldn't come in, he just wanted to wait.

Since Edgar had gone off to Somerset I'd hardly had anything to do with him. Even when he was home for the holidays, he just sloped against the verandah wall with his hands in his pockets, waiting for Mrs. Arbuthnot to tell him to take them out.

Edgar was tall now, much taller than I was, and sometimes I'd stop in fright because at a distance he could have been any Somerset boy with his boater gone skew and his satchel on his back, kicking at the gate to open it. If I could have been sure he was still the same as he used to be, I'd have called out. But I wasn't, and so I just pretended not to see him.

Anyway, Ma had begun to complain about Harding's Rest. It was high time I put that place behind me, she said, instead

of running up the hill like a handmaiden the moment I was
summoned. She had to wonder why a man like George Harding would even bother with a schoolgirl like me, now that
the half-wit was out of his hair. What did he want? And why
couldn't I just stick to Ruth Frank if I felt like some company?
The Franks were cultivated people, after all, and even though
that Sarah Frank had a mighty opinion of herself, one had to
hand it to them—when the Royal Country Club had invited
Roger Frank to join, he'd turned them down flat on principle.
Unlike someone else she might name.

She'd completely forgotten any pride she'd ever taken in
my father, or even in the Hardings and Harding's Rest. All
her enthusiasm now was for people like Mr. Ledson—people
who'd pulled themselves up by their bootstraps. Just look at
D. H. Lawrence—look what a mark he'd left on the world!

I found Edgar sloping against the wall with his hands in his
pockets.

"Edgar?" I said, as if I wasn't quite sure.

"Grandmother wants you to come for tea," he mumbled.
His voice had a croak in it now, and there were pimples on his
forehead. "Mrs. Arbuthnot's gone," he said quickly. "She's
not there anymore."

"Gone? Gone where?"

But he just gave his small shrug.

"Phin," I said, "tell Ma I've gone up to Ruth's."

"Hawu." He was still a minister and knew quite well how
to tell a fib from a lie.

"Hawu yourself," I said.

*

"Would you play for us now, dear?" said old Mrs. Harding
when the tea things were being cleared away. She seemed

madder than ever. Three times she'd asked who I was, and three times she'd said, "Now *that's* an unusual name!"

"I'm so sorry," I said. "I don't have my music with me." But the truth was that, except for banging things out to annoy Mr. Ledson, I hardly played at all anymore. Right from the start he'd expected more from the new grand piano, he said. "Can't you play a song we can all enjoy?" he'd say. Or "How long's this racket going to go on for, might I ask?"

And so, as soon as I heard his car coming into the garage, I'd start banging out scales. And when I'd had enough of that I'd fetch *The Scourge of the Swastika* or *House of Dolls* and lie on the couch reading. I knew that the sight of them would have him muttering about people who wouldn't put the past behind them, people who thought they were better than everyone else in the world.

"We *are* better," I'd mumble, but so softly that he'd have to turn his good ear and say, "Come again? *Come again?*" And then off he'd go to complain to Ma, and after supper she'd come to my room to ask if I thought I was making her life any easier, waving those books around like an avenging angel. Which only gave me the chance to point out that if we'd had to owe our lives to men like Mr. Ledson, we'd have landed in the gas chambers ourselves.

And so the war continued.

"I kept sending the boy to find you," said old Mrs. Harding. "But he told me you'd gone away."

"Just down the hill," I said. But there was something so lonely now in the sound of the words that I had to press my lips together to keep them from quivering. The afternoon was windy and grey, and there was something lonely about everything, even old Mrs. Harding's wanting me to play for her.

I felt sorry for her, somehow, and sorry for myself as well. "When is Mr. Harding coming back?" I asked.

No one answered, but without Mr. Harding waiting for me in his study, there seemed no point in my being there at all.

"Would you play for us now, dear?" said old Mrs. Harding again.

I stood up. "I'm sorry, Mrs. Harding, I have to go home now. I'll bring my music next time."

Edgar rocked back in his chair. All afternoon he'd said nothing except "please" and "thank you," and even then there'd been a new smirk on his face. "Want to go down to the summerhouse?" he mumbled, too softly for old Mrs. Harding to hear.

It was the first time he'd ever suggested anything, even a book to read, and I glanced quickly to see if he was still smirking. But he wasn't, he was blushing, and his pimples were purple. I knew perfectly well that he was only suggesting what normal boys suggested, and yet it was so ridiculous to be blushing myself because of Edgar that I trotted down into the garden and across the terrace as if it had been my idea in the first place.

"Where's she going?" old Mrs. Harding asked.

"Come," I called back, skipping down through the flower beds, rock to rock, and then standing at the bottom to watch him pick his way carefully down the steps. He stopped at the bottom, tall, spare, bony. If Ruth and I were to pass a boy like him on the street, we'd roll our eyes and make cutting remarks, even though we both longed for boys to follow us, I knew, any boys, even Edgar, although we never said so to each other, and everyone said we were snobs.

I went to sit on the summerhouse bench and he followed. "It's boring down here," I said.

He leaned forward, staring out over the lawn as if he were watching a game of cricket.

"Did Somerset expel you?" I said, trying to have things back the way they used to be.

"I hate them, I hate everyone there."

"I hate Mr. Ledson, too. I wish he'd be killed in a car crash, but of course he never will be."

"I used to wish everyone would be killed," Edgar said. "You, too."

"What?" I stared at him as if I'd been slapped. "Why me?" My lips were quivering again, and for what? For Edgar? I turned away, but suddenly tears were streaming down my cheeks. I covered my face with my hands and heaved into them, forgetting Edgar completely because, somehow, it was my father I was crying for, the dark, cold absence he had left me with. Until now, death seemed to have swallowed him into a mist, more like another sort of life than death itself. It was nothing like the Germans hunting you down and herding you off, looming out of the mist themselves. He was dead, truly dead, and it was cruel and horrible, and nothing I could do would ever make any difference.

And then suddenly, without warning, Edgar grabbed me by the shoulders and clamped his mouth over mine. It happened so quickly that for a moment I thought he really was trying to kill me because I couldn't breathe, my nose was blocked from all the crying. But the more I struggled the worse it got. He was snorting and heaving as if he were crying himself, and I had to reach up from behind and grab a handful of his wiry hair, pull it and pull it until at last he had to let go, and I fell forward, gasping in some air.

"It's not my fault," he said, moving off to the other side of the bench.

"What?" I was still heaving. "What did you say?"

But he wouldn't say it again, he wouldn't look at me either.

I jumped to my feet and came to stand in front of him. "*Whose* fault is it then? *Whose?*"

He tried to look away, but I kept moving in front of him, wherever he turned. I gave his shoulder a shove. "You're pathetic!" I shouted. "You're repulsive! And you're full of pimples! Ag! I'm probably going to catch them now!"

But it was impossible to insult Edgar. He just sat with his mouth open, like a dog. So I walked down the steps and around the bamboo to the small strip of grass where I used to hide.

"Cressida?" He was at the top of the steps. "What are you doing?"

"I'm waiting."

"Why?"

I knew he'd come down. I knew he'd do whatever I told him to now, like jumping out of the window or painting the walls of the house. "Come down here," I said.

He came creeping down and around to where I was, and then just stood there, looking into the bamboo. It always seemed alive in the wind, creaking and cracking, and Ma said there were rats' nests in there, and she'd never plant it in a garden herself, certainly not.

"First you must take off your trousers," I said.

He stared at me, dumb.

"Hurry up," I said. "I have to go soon."

He turned away and squatted to unlace his shoes, placing them neatly side by side. Then he took off his trousers and folded them on top of his shoes.

"Now lie down and shut your eyes."

He stretched out on the grass, white and bony and ridiculous in his shirt and socks and underpants.

"Your thing's sticking sideways," I said, stepping a little closer to have a look. "Ag! It's revolting!"

He covered it with his hands. "Touch it," he whispered, keeping his eyes closed tight.

"*What?*"

"Touch it."

My stomach lurched. Ruth and I made fun of the girls at school with their cheese-and-wine parties and the Somerset boys who went all the way with them. Except for Edwina, they were cheap, Ruth said, they'd do any disgusting thing boys asked them to. Just like Miranda, I said, and look where it got her. I often spoke of Miranda like this. I wanted Ruth to know how different we were, how different I was from all of them.

But now here I was myself, and even though it was only Edgar asking for something disgusting, my heart had begun to race at the thought of it. If he hadn't turned onto his side just then, I might have gone closer, I might have sat down next to him just to see if he'd ask again, forgetting completely who he was and why I'd made him take off his trousers in the first place.

Suddenly, I ran over to where he'd left them, and flung them high into the bamboo, his shoes after them. "There!" I shouted. "There! Who are you going to blame for that?"

He wasn't listening. He was curled around himself the way he used to when he fell off his bike. And he was whimpering, crying like a baby. "Ah! Ah! Ah!"

Chapter 17

I didn't go back to Harding's Rest until six weeks later, when Mr. Harding summoned me himself. Phineas brought me the note, careful that Ma didn't see him. "Master Edgar he fail again," he said. "Hawu, shame, he not so clever like you." There was nothing Phineas didn't know about the big house from their servants. So how could he not have found out about Edgar and me and his trousers in the bamboo?

I put on my sandals and slammed past him out of the house. All this time I'd been keeping a lookout for Mr. Harding's car, for Mr. Harding himself, and now, just as I'd forgotten about him—just as I'd settled onto the couch with *Julius Caesar*—there was the envelope with CRESSIDA written in his dark blue ink.

He didn't look up when I came into the study, he didn't even say, "Ah, Cressida, there you are!" So I stood where I was, waiting in the familiar gloom—nothing really different

about it, and yet nothing the same either. For one thing, he
was wearing a hat again, but a smaller one this time, and he
wore it at an angle, without a veil. For another, I was full of
accusations myself. All the way up the hill they'd been rising
in my chest—questions he wouldn't be able to answer, things
I had to say myself.

"Well, what do you have to say for yourself?" he said at
last. His voice seemed damp and muffled, as if it came from
too far down his throat. "I blame myself," he went on before
I could answer. "I should have remembered that you are your
mother's daughter after all."

"My mother?" My heart leaped now for Ma. It twisted itself into an ache for her slave bangle and ankle bracelet, and for
the way she'd come in to tell me that Mr. Ledson was taking us
all to Giant's Peak for the Christmas holidays—everyone, even
Miranda and her family. She'd gabbled it out so quickly that I
knew she was scared I'd make a fuss and refuse to go.

"My mother doesn't even want me to come here anymore," I said fiercely.

"Of course she doesn't, of course she doesn't. For God's
sake, Cressida, come and sit down. Why are you still standing
over there?"

But I was remembering everything I'd always hated about
him, and I was hating him all over again. If he wanted to wear
a hat in front of me, so much the better. I hated his head
as well.

"Well then take your medicine standing up. It was Mrs. Arbuthnot who warned me, you know. She said that if I left you
two together it would eventually come to this." He sighed. "If
it were anyone else, I'd have welcomed such an eventuality for
that little twerp. But you! *You*, Cressida! This is not what I had
in mind for you!"

"But I didn't!" I shouted, my throat closing up with rage.

"You want me to believe that Edgar was so overcome with passion that he flung his trousers into the bamboo? Like this?" He took his hat by the brim and flung it furiously across the room. And then there was his head, bandaged across the bad side, even over the bad eye.

He leaned back in the chair and let out another long, damp sigh. Whatever Ma said, it was impossible to think of him with a bride or a mistress, it was revolting. "Pardon me for calumnizing your mother," he said. "It was wrong of me. Would you forgive me?"

But I wouldn't look at him, I wouldn't sit down either.

"Blame it on this if you like." He patted the bandage. "It has put me in a very bad temper."

"What happened?"

"Oh, they tried something new. Too soon to tell. Well," he said, reaching for his pipe, "back to the matter at hand. As I say, I blame myself for this. I should have left Edgar where I found him. It was a showy act of charity on my part, vainglorious and sentimental."

"But I threw his trousers as a joke," I said quickly. "I told him to take them off as a joke, and then I just threw them."

"That's the whole story?" He twisted around to stare at me.

I shrugged. Nothing I could say would make any difference now, and anyway, what was the whole story? Even if I wanted to tell him, where would I find the words for what I hardly understood myself? What had begun to sink with me into sleep over the weeks, filling me with longing, and also with shame? And for what? For Edgar? It was impossible.

"Cressida, listen to me now. Edgar is my brother Charles's little bastard, about that there is no doubt. His mother was married to one of Charles's good friends. Married women, as you may have gathered, were Charles's particular specialty." He tilted his head to stare hard at me.

I waited, staring back.

"When her husband returned, wounded, from the war and found her great with child, he made her choose—throw the baggage out when it was born, or be thrown out herself."

"Oh," I said, wondering whether Ma would have thrown me out like baggage.

"The usual story," he went on. "Stillborn, they said. And, of course, there was some relief in that. It was only years later, when the mother was on her deathbed, that I found out otherwise. It would all sound like something out of Dickens were it not for the fact that Edgar himself is so unsuited to the role of hero. Or of lover, for that matter. Ha!" He sat forward as if waiting for an answer.

"Shame," I mumbled.

"Shame? Did I hear you say 'shame,' Cressida? Where, pray, lies the shame? With my brother? With Edgar's mother? With Edgar himself? Surely not! Surely you're not the sort of person who would blame the child for the sins of his father?"

"I only meant——"

He sighed. "I know perfectly well what you meant. But you were committing a vulgar misuse of a splendid and ancient word in the way of shopgirls and motor-car mechanics. I expect more of you."

My face and ears were on fire now. And yet even as I told myself I was free to leave, that I could just turn around and leave the house and never come back, I stood where I was, dumb.

"Look, my dear," he said, "the fact is I cannot bear to see you throw yourself away on the likes of Edgar. His pedigree may be exemplary, give or take benefit of clergy, but just look at the product! Promise me, Cressida, that you won't squander yourself on the likes of Edgar."

"I *won't*," I shouted suddenly. "I never *would* have! I *didn't*!"

"Good, good. Well then, how shall we proceed? Edgar is to be home now, as you probably know. He'll be going to Delaney with all the other morons, and I shall engage a private tutor for him. I'd like to get him through JC at least before I turn him out into the world."

"I don't want to tutor Edgar," I said quickly. "My mother never wanted me to tutor him in the first place."

He threw back his head and gave out one of his hideous roars. "Ah, Cressida, tell me this—does your mother know you're up here?"

"No."

"Well, perhaps it should remain our secret. Perhaps you can slip away from time to time and come up for tea?"

I nodded, but how did he think I could just slip away when anyone could see me going up and down the hill, even Mr. Ledson? And anyway, why would I want to? And, even if I did, what about Ruth? When I'd told her about Edgar clamping his mouth over mine, she'd said, "Ag! Sis! Edgar! That's revolting!" And then we'd done Edgar imitations for each other, and even Mr. Harding imitations, and she'd brought out her father's hat and an old tulle ballet skirt for a veil.

"We're all going to Giant's Peak for the Christmas holidays," I said.

"Then come over when you return." He sat forward. "Indulge me in this, Cressida. Would you mind that badly?"

Chapter 18

Ruth's family was going to be at Giant's Peak as well. They went there every year, she said, and, yay, we'd be there together. I tried to join in, but all I could think of was Mrs. Frank and Ma, Mrs. Frank and Mr. Ledson. When I went to Ruth's house, Mrs. Frank always stopped to say hello on her way out of her study, and once she even smiled and said, "My word, Cressida, but you're the image of your late father!" She was haughty and proud and elegant, and she never mentioned Ma, not even to ask how she was doing these days. So how was I going to bear it when Ma started showing off for her? and worse would be Mr. Ledson.

I drove up with Miranda and Derek, and all the way Miranda complained about Ma. Could I imagine, she said, Ma wouldn't even allow her to bring the children over for a swim on Sundays because they made too much noise and ruined Uncle Albert's peace and quiet. She tossed her head. Her hair was peroxided now, and she wore the same sort of silver snake bangle as Ma. So there was going to be Miranda to keep away from Mrs. Frank, too, and Derek picking his teeth with a match, and the closer we got to Giant's Peak, the more I wished I'd refused to go after all.

Mr. Ledson had reserved two blocks of rooms in their own bungalow, with me at the far end. "Drinks time!" he called out when we arrived. "What's your poison, Derek? Girls, your mother's inside unpacking."

"I've got to unpack too," Miranda said, leaving her boys to shriek and slide along the verandah.

"Quiet!" Mr. Ledson barked at them, stopping them dead.

All the way up in the car I'd longed to shout at them like that, but Miranda was as scared of them as she used to be of me. "Please, boys," she'd plead. "Please!" And when they didn't listen, she just gave me a sheepish smile. So now there they were, crying off to her room, and there was Mr. Ledson, turning to me and rolling his eyes as if we both knew how much they might benefit from the strap.

"Your aunt will be here tomorrow," he said.

"Bunch?" It was impossible. "How?"

"Coming down on the bus. We have to pick her up in Escourt."

"Ah, there you are," Ma said when I burst into her room. "What do you think? This one or that one for tonight?" She held out the dresses by the hangers.

"Ma!" I said. "Why is Bunch coming? Why?"

"Are you starting already? Before you've even unpacked?"

"But *why*, Ma? This was supposed to be *our* holiday!"

She sighed. "It certainly wasn't my doing, I can assure you."

"Whose, then?" But I knew already. Mr. Ledson. He was so

pleased with himself for taking us all on a holiday we wouldn't have been able to afford without him that he'd even asked me to bring a friend.

"But why should Mr. Ledson care if Bunch comes? Why?"

"Because he answered the bloody phone when she rang, that's why!" she snapped. "And if I hear any more whining about it, you can get on the bus yourself and go home." She took a furious look in the long wardrobe mirror and hung the dresses back on the door.

"The Franks are also coming tomorrow," I said miserably.

She turned to look at me. "What?"

"They always come here for the Christmas holidays."

"Well, now that's something, isn't it?" she said. "I might have known the Franks would frequent a place like this. How long did they say they were coming for?"

"Three weeks."

"Hmm." She folded her arms and stared into the wardrobe mirror. "Did you know there's going to be a fancy dress on New Year's Eve? We're all going to have to put our thinking caps on." She smiled. "Sarah and Roger Frank, hey? Well, that's something, isn't it?"

"Where's Bunch going to stay?" I said quickly.

She came over then and put her hands on my shoulders. "Look, darling," she said, "Uncle Albert tried everything he knew, even crossing their palms with silver, but they're completely full up. So I've asked them to bring down a Ping-Pong bat for you. I can't imagine she's still at it, but just in case, you know."

Chapter 19

Mrs. Frank wouldn't be caught dead in fancy dress, Ruth said, but her father was going to go as the Rajah of Knockadoor and wanted Ruth and me to dress up in saris and go as his two Responses. Mr. Frank loved jokes like that. He had nicknames for everyone, even for me. Hello, Cressilumps, he'd say. And then Mrs. Frank would shake her head and tell me that Cressida was a beautiful old name and had I read *Troilus and Cressida*? Had I read Chaucer?

And so I felt at home with them right from the start. And, when Bunch arrived, and Mrs. Frank asked if I wouldn't prefer to move in with Ruth, it was as if she also understood that I didn't belong down there with the others. "I remember your aunt as a girl," she said. "Your father was always very kind to her, you know. One would see them together at our Saturday matinees. I'm so glad to see she hasn't been forgotten."

She never mentioned Ma unless she had to, and when they walked past our table in the dining room she just gave a nod, never a smile. So I knew right from the start that she couldn't stand the sight of Ma, and although I couldn't stand the sight of her myself—although I'd sit proudly on the verandah with the Franks, drinking a shandy with Ruth as they all trooped past— still, there'd be an ache across my heart at the sight of her, I couldn't help it.

And so I went over to their table to say hello. But Ma just rolled her eyes and said, "Look, the Queen of Sheba is gracing us with her presence!" And they all joined in, even the children. "Queen of Sheba! Queen of Sheba!" they chanted. And after that, the ache was gone, and I didn't go over to them again.

When Ruth and I came out in our saris, red dots on our foreheads and our skin dark from the sun, Sammy the barman stopped in amazement. Mrs. Frank had made our costumes with material from the Indian shop in town. She'd made Mr. Frank's turban as well, and pinned a brooch on the front of it, and adjusted his red satin sash. "Turn!" she had barked at us, and we'd turned like a trio of dancers. "Now the other way, please—Ruth, for God's sake, stand up straight!"

Mrs. Frank took everything seriously, Ruth said, even cartoons. And could I imagine having to live with it? Could I? She said it loudly enough for Mrs. Frank to overhear, but she never seemed to take Ruth's complaints seriously. Anyway, I could see they weren't really complaints at all, they were more like a game they all played with each other, and I longed to be able to join in.

"Ready, girls?" Mrs. Frank said. "All right, in we go!"

Through the double doors we went and down the middle of the dining room. As we passed Ma's table, Mr. Ledson looked up and shouted, "Hey! There's Sheba! Sheba, come over here! Let's have a good look at you!

"You're going as a coolie girl?" he said when I went to stand at their table. "Whose idea was that?"

People at the next table turned to each other, and there were Indian waiters listening, too. "We never use that word in our family," I said.

"What word?" he demanded. "What word?"

But Bunch had jumped up now and was dancing from foot to foot. She was wearing a pair of bloomers on her head, with donkey's ears coming out of the openings. "Two guesses, Cresses!" she shouted. "No clues anyone!"

"Quiet, Bunch!" Ma said. "Keep it down, please!" She herself was wearing false eyelashes and bright red lipstick, and she'd painted a beauty spot on one cheek.

"Coolie?" said Mr. Ledson. "What's wrong with coolie?"

"Ma," I said quickly, "what are you wearing?"

"Give up?" Bunch cried. "I'm Bottom the Weaver! And Miranda's Titania! *My* idea! Now you have to guess the others!"

"What are you going as, Ma?" I said again.

"Irma la Deuce!" shouted Mr. Ledson. "You think you're so clever and you can't work that out?" He was wearing his golf cap at an angle, and Ma's red scarf knotted at his neck, with a black moustache painted under his enormous red nose.

"La *Douce*!" Ma said. "Irma la *Douce*!"

"Who's Irma la Douce?" I asked. But I didn't want to know. "Are you just wearing your swimming costume?"

"And my fishnet stockings," said Miranda.

"Here's to my Irma!" Mr. Ledson held up his champagne glass. "We're starting early. Want to join us, Miss Coolie?"

I shook my head. If Ma was going to parade onto the dance floor in a swimming costume and fishnet stockings I'd rather go back to the room. Except what would I say to Mrs. Frank? What would I say to any of them?

"As of tomorrow," Ma said, "you'll come back and sit with us. It's one thing to share a room with the Frank girl because your aunt is here, quite another to live and die with them." She put a cigarette into a cigarette holder and held it ready for Mr. Ledson to light.

"The cigarette holder's for Irma la Douce too," Bunch said cozily. "We had to borrow it from Mrs. Keen-Patterson."

"*We* didn't borrow it from anyone," Ma said. "Brenda Keen-Patterson lent it to *me*."

*

All through the judging I wondered how I would tell the Franks that I had to go back to our table the next day. "Ready, Cressilumps?" Mr. Frank said. "Pay attention now, Chopsticks, we're on next."

"The Rajah of Knockadoor and his two Responses," announced Mr. du Plessis.

"Eyes down, girls," Mrs. Frank said. "Remember, two paces behind, please."

And then out went Mr. Frank, striding slowly around the dance floor while we walked behind, and people clapped.

"Tweedledee and Tweedledum," shouted Mr. du Plessis. "Bottom the Weaver and Titania. Robin Hood. The old woman in the shoe. Irma la Douce——"

Ma walked out onto the dance floor in her high-heeled sandals, swinging her hips and waving Mrs. Keen-Patterson's cigarette holder. She'd knotted a chiffon scarf around her waist for a skirt, and as she walked it swung open so you could see right up her legs. Some of the men put their fingers in their mouths and whistled, but most of them just smiled and clapped, and I saw Mrs. Keen-Patterson lean over and say something to Mrs. Sutherland across the table, and they both rolled their eyes.

Next to Ma, Mr. Ledson looked like a dwarf. He always looked like a dwarf when she wore high heels, but now he was sweating, and his moustache was beginning to run. All around the dining room people were giggling, and so I tried to giggle too. I threw back my head and laughed, and Ruth joined in.

Only Mrs. Frank paid no attention. She dug into her bag for a cigarette, then she lit it, looking up at the ceiling as she blew out the smoke. And so maybe Ma thought she wasn't noticing when she turned and gave Mr. Frank a big wink. But just as he was blowing her a kiss, Mrs. Frank swerved around and said, "I thought I'd made myself perfectly clear, Roger." Her large white bosom was heaving, and when the band struck up and Mr. Frank asked her for the first dance, she didn't even bother to answer him.

"She's always like this," Ruth whispered. "Don't say I didn't warn you." But I knew already that nothing would ever be the same again for me. And just as I was thinking of a way to say it was really all Mr. Ledson's fault, because who'd given Ma slave bangles and ankle bracelets in the first place?—there was Mr. Frank strolling away to ask Ma for the next dance.

So that was that for Mrs. Frank. She smashed her cigarette into the ashtray and stood up. "Ruth," she said, "kindly tell your father that I've gone to the room."

"But, Ma, they haven't even done the judging. It isn't even midnight yet!"

"Midnight!" she spat out, turning to go. But then suddenly Mr. Ledson was blocking her path. "Want to give it a go, Sarah?" he said, his smile disappearing under his nose. "The night is still young."

She stared at him as if he were a servant who didn't belong in the house. "No thank you," she said. "I do not wish to 'give it a go.'" And she swept off in her long black dress, out of the dining room.

He stood for a few moments, staring after her. But Ruth and I were giggling so helplessly, covering our mouths with our saris and snorting into them, that he came over and gave me a clip on the shoulder. "You," he said. "Get up! Come on! On your feet! You're going to dance."

"I don't want to dance, thank you," I said, still laughing. "I'm staying here with Ruth."

He took hold of the back of my chair and tipped it forward. "I said get up. You're going to dance whether you like it or not."

People were turning to watch us now. "I don't *want* to dance!" I said, not laughing anymore. But it was hopeless, he had me by the arm and was leading me out onto the dance floor. "Mr. Ledson," I said, trying to pull away. "I told you, I don't want to!"

"Don't you 'Mr. Ledson' me," he growled, putting his hand around my waist and moving me into the middle of the dance floor. "Take my hand! Move your feet!" He swung me out hard, caught me again, swung me this way, that way, so that my legs tangled up in the sari and I had to grab on to him to stop myself from falling.

"Not much of a dancer, are you?" he said. "Not like your mother. Look at her making a spectacle of herself!"

I looked. She was dipping back, swirling around, winding her legs between Mr. Frank's, and then stalking across the dance floor with him, perfectly in step.

"We'll show them," Mr. Ledson muttered, holding my arm out straight like theirs. But just then the music changed to a slow song and the lights went down. He pulled me so close I had to cough with the smell of his sweat, and his horrible breath hot on my neck.

"Show them what?" I tried to say, but my throat had tightened around the words, and they came out in a squeak.

Behind us, Ma was breaking into one of her laughs, and Mr. Frank took her by the arm and was leading her off the dance floor. They sailed past us and out onto the verandah arm in arm, in time to the music.

Mr. Ledson stopped right in the middle of the dance floor to watch them go.

"Mr. Ledson ——"

"Didn't I warn you?" he said between his teeth. And suddenly he had my arm in his grip again and was pulling me across the dance floor and out onto the verandah, stopping only for a moment to look up and down before plunging us down the steps and out onto the dark terrace.

I could have tried to pull my arm away, I could have shouted for help, but it was just like being in one of my nightmares—even if he'd tried to murder me right there, I couldn't say a word.

He pulled me farther out onto the grass. There was no one there, no sound except the crickets and the voices coming from inside. And then suddenly he stopped dead, staring ahead. I stared too. There, caught in the light from the verandah, was the top of Mr. Frank's turban.

It took me a while to see what they were doing, but then I saw Ma's scarf lying on the grass, and Ma and Mr. Frank deep in the shadow of the verandah wall, wrapped around each other, kissing.

"Mr. Ledson!" I managed to whisper. But I'd hardly got the words out before he clamped his hand over my mouth. Inside, the band was still playing, normal people were there doing normal things in there. Soon they'd be announcing the winners, and people would be coming out for a breath of fresh air, walking down onto the terrace with their glasses of champagne. "Ma!" I tried to shout, jerking my head away.

But Mr. Ledson grabbed me hard and swung me around. "You watching this, Muriel?" he shouted. And then he clamped his mouth over mine. It was wet and hot and stinking, and my stomach lurched into my throat.

"I say, Ledson!" said Mr. Frank.

But that only made Mr. Ledson pull me closer and shove his hips against me, snorting his horrible breath all over me. He was doing it because he hated me, I knew that, and because he hated Ma now as well.

"Albert!"

And then, at last, he let me go. He pushed me forward so that I nearly staggered into Ma. "Have a good look at your mother!" he shouted. "Proud of her? See what you'll be yourself one day!"

"Now look here, Ledson," said Mr. Frank, "this was just a bit of fun——"

"Fun? Fun? You think I can't see for myself what you've been after the whole bloody week?" He stepped around me, right up to Mr. Frank. "Fun you say? Don't think you can get round *me* with your slimy Jew-boy tricks!" And suddenly he hit Mr. Frank so hard that he staggered back, holding his nose.

"Albert!" Ma came into the light. Her lipstick was smudged and her mascara was running with tears. "Cressida," she sobbed, "go back to your room!"

I picked up my sari and ran. And the more I ran, the more it felt as if Mr. Ledson was running after me. So I fell and cut my knee, and then scrambled up again, grabbing up my sari and making off across the grass and down through the rockeries, stumbling and falling and sobbing until I burst into the room. And there was Ruth, already in her shorty pajamas, brushing her teeth.

Chapter 20

So that is how I came to be back at Harding's Rest. It was hard to know whose idea it was really—Ma's, because she wanted to save her marriage, or Mr. Ledson's, because he'd found a way to blame me after all, or even Mr. Harding's, because I'd be doing him a favour, he said, old Mrs. Harding was in need of companionship and would welcome my return.

At first I was supposed to stay in Mrs. Arbuthnot's old room, but as soon as the servant closed the door I knew that it would be impossible. The whole room smelled sour like her, and also sweet with her horrible wild gardenia scent. I ran to the windows and pushed them wide open, but it didn't make any difference. She was everywhere, even the antimacassars still had some of her hairs on them. But how could I tell Mr. Harding this? When Phineas had dropped me off at the front door, he'd come out himself to greet me. "Ah, Cressida!" he'd said, taking my arm. "My mother has been asking for you every hour."

Standing with him in the dim light of the hall, with its smell of floor polish and skins and pipe tobacco, I was as happy then as I'd ever been at the top of the flamboyant all those years before. Mrs. Arbuthnot was gone, and Mr. Harding was going to pay me to be old Mrs. Harding's companion. He was going to put money into a building society every month, he said, and if I wanted to take it out, all I had to do was go down there myself. And if I was one of those people who saved for an uncertain future, I could do that as well. It was all up to me.

I stared out of the window at the old servants' quarters, thinking of how Mrs. Arbuthnot must have stared out like this herself. She must have watched me coming across to the big house and wondered, as I'd wondered myself, why Mr. Harding would want me there at all.

He listened carefully when I went down to the study. Without his bandages, he almost had a proper forehead now, and his bad eye had been lifted up a bit so that, even though it still seemed too wide open, at least it wasn't staring in the wrong direction.

"You'd prefer to be back in your old quarters, Cressida?" he said. He smiled so that I'd know he wasn't cross. "Well, I'm afraid that's impossible. You see, I've put Edgar in there."

"Edgar?"

"I wanted him out of my sight for a while. Perhaps I should have put him on a ship and sent him to the North Pole. But, as it is, one of his tutors is living over there with him, and he has a timetable to adhere to, so we'll see what that will accomplish."

Ma had left everything behind in the old servants' quarters when she'd married Mr. Ledson, even my father's wicker chair. So now Edgar was sitting on our couch and sleeping in our beds, and all I had was Mrs. Arbuthnot's antimacassars.

"I'll tell you what," Mr. Harding said, "I shall have the servants prepare a different room for you. I'll have to alert my mother or she'll think she's seeing a ghost. Can you stand the company of Mrs. Arbuthnot's ghost for another night or so until the servants get it ready?"

*

And so that is how I came to be in Mr. Charles's old room. Until now it had been used as a storeroom, Mr. Harding said, not because old Mrs. Harding had read too many novels, but because it was where Mr. Harding himself had lain all those months and months after he'd come back from the war, and what with that and his mother wandering in and out in a delirium of grief, he'd decided, once he was back on his feet, to take up residence in the north wing, which could be closed off from the rest of the house, to give himself a modicum of privacy.

As soon as I was alone in the room, I spread my arms, as happy as I'd been in the hall. It was large and light, with green watered silk on the walls, stained now, but lovely. And there were French doors that opened on to the upstairs verandah, and any time I wanted to I could go out there and sit on the verandah wall, at least until old Mrs. Harding came along to tell me to get down, it was dangerous. Her own room was at the other end of the verandah, with French doors permanently fastened open because she liked to wake up with the birds, she said, even if they were only Indian mynahs.

She was always on the lookout for me, poking her head out and then shuffling along to my room. One day she brought me a small leather box. Inside was a gold-and-garnet pendant on a delicate gold chain. It needed a young neck like mine, she said, and no, no, it was hers to give and mine to take, and she'd hear no more about it.

As soon as she was gone I took it down to Mr. Harding because what if he saw me wearing it? But when I held it out to him, he just frowned at me and said, "What is your objection? Does the gift not please you?"

And so I was forced to remind him about the silver spoon and forks, and before I could even get to the part about Ma bringing them right back, he was banging out his pipe on the elephant foot, saying, "If she chooses to give away her jewelry, or the household silver, or anything she damned well pleases, that is her prerogative. Dismissed."

I went back upstairs and out onto the verandah. Then I climbed onto the wall, standing up to see if I could find our house down the hill. And yes, there it was among the trees, the green of the roof and a bit of the swimming bath as well. But seeing it only reminded me of Mr. Ledson, and of Ma, everything I couldn't bear to go back to.

Every Thursday now Ma picked me up from choir practice and took me down to the Matador for a mixed grill. And then, as soon as she'd had a glass of sangria, she'd start up on many a slip in life, and one day I'd understand, *I* had my whole life ahead of me, which was more than she could say for herself.

When I pointed out that she had her whole life ahead of her too, although maybe a bit less of it than there'd been before, she didn't ask if I thought I was being funny. She just swirled the fruit around in her glass and poured herself some more sangria, saying if I thought what she was going through was a picnic, I'd be quite mistaken. And by then I'd be tilting my panama so I didn't have to see her lips begin to quiver, and the way she dug into her bag for a hanky to blow her nose. There was something about her now that was almost as revolting to me as Mr. Ledson, and I didn't ever want her to mention his name to me again.

"Darling," she whispered urgently, "we should keep our voices down. Rory McCloughlin might be pretending to busy himself behind the bar but he's not fooling me. Before you know, it'll be all round Film Society."

"What?" I said coldly, turning to her. "The picnic you're not having?"

"That I've had to give up my courses at varsity, for instance," she whispered.

I shrugged. "So what? That's hardly big news. Did you ever actually read any of those books you kept waving around?"

"He won't let me, he hardly lets me out of his sight now."

"Who? Mr. McCloughlin?"

She gave me a sharp look. "Albert."

So now she was trying out "Albert" on me, and next thing she'd be suggesting I try it out for myself. There was nothing she wouldn't try to slide around when it came to Mr. Ledson, even me.

I stood up. "I can't even go over to the Franks' anymore because of you," I said loudly.

She put her finger wildly to her lips.

"But everyone knows already! Is there anyone in town who *doesn't* know what happened with Mr. Frank? And what about Mr. Charles? What about all the others you've tried to inveigle?"

"Cressida!"

"It's only because of Dad I'm at Harding's Rest in the first place! You certainly can't think it's because of you!"

And suddenly, shouting the words at her, it was as if the

truth had been waiting all those years for me to find it out. "Dad was nothing like you!" I said, tears storming down my face now. "You're slimy and cheap, and so is that vile creature you married! I wish I could squash you both like slugs!"

"Rory!" she called out desperately. "How much do I owe you? So sorry, we have to dash!"

But as she was digging in her bag for the money, I grabbed my school case and ran out of the door and up Tudor Lane to Joubert Street. It was lit up now, full of people going home from work. My bus was at the bus stop and it was almost full. "Sorry," I said, pushing to the front of the queue and jumping on. "Sorry!" I clambered up the stairs and fell into the last European seat.

And then, as soon as I came into the house, Mr. Harding burst out of his study, his whole head on fire. "Just *what* is the meaning of this?" he bellowed, standing right over me. "*How* did you get home?" His eye was wild and he looked as if he'd hit me. But with the hall all lit up and the dogs wagging around my legs, I just dropped my case and threw my arms around his neck, sobbing against his chest.

Chapter 21

All this time Edgar had been sliding around the edges like a tall, thin shadow. If he saw me coming, he put his head down and plunged his hands into his pockets, walking away as if he had somewhere to go. After a while I took to crossing his path deliberately, and then swerving away before he or Mr. Harding could think I might want anything to do with him.

He was allowed to come and go at the big house whenever he wished, but he hardly ever did. And so every evening Mr. Harding and I dined alone because old Mrs. Harding preferred a tray in her room at six o'clock with me reading *The Forsyte Saga* while she ate. She had been reading it for more than fifteen years, Mr. Harding said. He'd bought all three volumes for her, but who could have imagined it would have come to this? She knew that family better than her own. He could even conjure up some sympathy for Mrs. Arbuthnot, who'd had to read it night after night.

"But I like it," I said. "I love it."

"The books? Oh yes, they'll hold up for the first or even the second time around. But fifteen years of social satire?" He gave one of his laughs. "At least my father put his foot down when she started trying to concoct a dynasty here. She was always one for cultivating nostalgia."

"For what?"

"Oh, the family crest, the country seat, that sort of thing. Pure invention, of course. Probably saw herself as Irene. Mind you, if it hadn't been for her beauty, she'd have been left where my father found her, playing the organ at St. Thomas's church and giving piano lessons in the afternoons."

I stared at him. Sometimes he would lead me into elaborate jokes like this and then, without warning, burst into one of his dreadful guffaws. I hated it and hated myself for being taken in again and again. So I waited to see what would come next. He was always telling me to wait. "No, no, no!" he'd bark. "Wait until you've tasted the wine before you swallow it!"

We sat at either end of the long dining-room table. It was dark and gloomy in there, like the hall. On my first night he'd suggested gently that I might prefer to wear something a little less depressing than my school uniform to dinner. He himself was accustomed to changing for dinner, he said. But all I had to change into were Ma's old dresses. She'd packed them up quickly as I was leaving even though I'd told her not to bother, I'd never be wearing them anyway.

But there I sat now in her yellow dress and bolero, breathing in the stale smell of her Black Narcissus.

"So you see," he said. "You're not the only one who has had to contend with the legacy of a beautiful mother."

"What happened to Mrs. Arbuthnot?" I asked quickly. Somehow I couldn't bear talking about Ma with him. I wanted everything about her separated from Harding's Rest, and from Mr. Harding as well.

He rang the bell for pudding. "She found herself a widower down at the beachfront. Perhaps she'd got wind of the fact that I was looking for a replacement."

I looked up for a joke again. But Shadrak was bringing in the fruit salad and ice cream, and when I had served it, Mr. Harding looked down the table and said, "Someone has to run this house, Cressida, you must see that. And I also have you to think about now."

"Me?"

"Certainly. A young woman up here, alone, with an old woman, a cripple, and a half-wit—it won't do at all, I'm afraid."

"But I don't care!" I said loudly. "Why can't *I* be the housekeeper?"

He laughed, and I looked at him, trying to remember how that head had once been the whole war to me. They were separated now, he and the war, and I could even feel sorry for him, not so much for what had happened to him as for the way my stomach had turned at the sight of him chewing or swallowing or wiping his chin. Nothing about his head mattered to me now, and it didn't matter how many times I stared into the old snapshots, I'd never be able to see him any other way. I never wanted to either.

"You are not cut out to be a servant," he said. "And clearly this house cannot run itself. Fruit salad and ice cream night after night? And when is the last time there was cake for tea, may I ask?"

I looked down into my empty bowl. He was right. I had no interest in the kitchen or in cakes. All I wanted was to keep things the way they were. Everything was freer now, even my dreams. The Germans had slipped out of them before I'd even noticed. And I could switch off the light and lie in the dark full of hope for the future, whatever it was going to be.

"At the end of the year you'll be finished with school and off to the university," he said. "And then what?"

"But I don't want to go to university!" On Fridays I was allowed a second glass of wine and it always made me forget what I should keep to myself.

"Don't be ridiculous. What do you have in mind? Working in the shop with your sister?"

I shook my head miserably. The truth was I had nothing in mind except, somehow, to leap the years between now and when I'd be able to have it all behind me.

"If you don't care about my wishes, you might at least consider your father's."

"My father?"

"He was an educated man, with educated tastes and an educated upbringing. It would certainly have been what he would have wanted for you. As I am in loco parentis, your mother notwithstanding, I intend you to make good on my investment."

"But *why?*"

"Why?" he roared, his face flushing instantly. "Because you are my brother's legacy, that's why! Accident or no, he is the one who orphaned you and I owe your father a debt I can never repay." He rang the bell furiously and stood up. "Coffee?"

Every night there was coffee in the lounge after dinner. Tonight, I knew, he'd want to talk about *The Guns of Navarone*. He was taking Edgar and me to the cinema tomorrow, and he always wanted me to know more about a story or a film than

anyone else. He wanted me to know so much about everything
that I'd forgotten what I used to want to know for myself.

I poured the coffee in silence. If all I was to him was a debt
to my father, then why had he bothered to see me as a rogue
cub all those years ago? Why had he even asked me what my
dreams were for the future? If he asked me now I'd tell him
they had nothing to do with what he wanted for me—that
what I wanted for myself was something much more magnif-
icent than university, something I'd be able to take without
asking. As soon as I found out what it was.

"Cressida," he said, touching my hand lightly as he put
back the sugar tongs. "It's for your own sake, you know that,
don't you?"

I turned my head away. Suddenly my eyes were filling with
tears. It could happen these days even when I was happy.

"Would you play the Beethoven for me after coffee?" he
asked. I was taking lessons again, practicing every day, although
I would have gladly given that up too. But as long as I was
at Harding's Rest I had no choice but to improve myself in
the ways Mr. Harding wanted me to. Being able to play a
Beethoven sonata was like being able to acquit oneself well on
the tennis court, he said. So now there were tennis lessons as
well—every Saturday afternoon at the Royal Country Club.
And on Sunday afternoons, when he was out riding, I had to
catch the bus with Ruth to the Jewish Club to play junior dou-
bles there.

But first I had to ring her gate bell, and then wait there like
a servant for her to come out. And even though she pretended
it was because her mother was rehearsing and didn't want to
be disturbed, I knew Mrs. Frank didn't want me in the house
at all anymore. But when I told Mr. Harding I'd prefer to give

up the Jewish Club altogether, he just shook his head. I was a Jew in a world of Gentiles, he said, something of which my father had never needed reminding.

"How did my father's accident happen?" I asked casually, stirring my coffee. "I mean was it really an accident?"

He gave out one of his sighs, and for a while I thought he might change the subject. He often did this, and then it was no use trying to bring it back. But now he sat forward, his elbows on his knees, and began to fill his pipe. And I knew I'd hear the proper story at last.

Chapter 22

"I wasn't there, of course," Mr. Harding said. "But from what I've heard, it had all the makings of French farce, always Charles's specialty. Still, women would persist in hurling themselves at him, and your mother, I'm afraid, was no exception. In this case, she had written him a letter, which your father came upon. So off he stormed, letter in hand, to confront Charles on the golf course.

"Charles and your father were in the same year at Cambridge, and often played golf together on a Saturday afternoon. In fact, Charles was the one who'd got your father into the club in the first place over some pretty stiff objections. So when your father came storming up, demanding an explanation, Charles was caught off guard. And then, once the letter was brandished, he tried laughing the whole thing off as a fling.

"Which I believe it was, at least for him. The whole thing seems to have been confined to one evening, some sort of party my mother had thrown during the war. Charles had never met your mother before—we moved in rather different social circles—but there she was suddenly, a dark-haired beauty, and he took her down to the summerhouse to show her the moon and the stars. As far as he was concerned that was the size of it. Until your father came storming up with that letter.

"It seems that this wasn't the first letter she'd written, and that Charles had ignored them all. He told your father this, thinking that would be an end to it. Charles was lacking in many things, but imagination was, perhaps, the greatest of them all. He was confined, if you will, by the limits of his own ability to feel, and being incapable of a grand passion himself, could never take seriously anyone else's. In this case, there was both a woman pleading and threatening and also your father, who happened to adore her with all the passion of a quiet man.

"He had married your mother against everyone's advice and certainly against his parents' wishes, to that I can certainly attest. But he was unregenerate, and, from what I gather, had plucked her—a raving beauty, a foot taller than he and considerably younger—from a rather meager little flat on the beachfront, where her father sold risqué magazines in a little shop downstairs. So now here she was, the prize he had fought for, accusing his friend of fathering her unborn child. It is my conviction, by the way, that your father knew perfectly well that this wasn't possible. In the event, you were born far too large and far too soon to have belonged to Charles. But you were not the point in this matter, I'm afraid. She was."

He leaned back in the chair and closed his eyes as if that was all there was to say.

"But how did it happen?" I asked. "The accident?"

He sighed. "Your father was a man possessed. At some point in the mêlée that followed, he managed to pull an iron out of Charles's golf bag and began flailing it around. People came running, of course, but Charles, still hoping, I suppose, that he could turn it all into a lark, at least for the purposes of the audience, grabbed an iron for himself and began to fence. He was taller and considerably larger than your father, and I don't know quite how it happened, but at one point your father turned to look behind him midswing, and that's when Charles's iron came down across his skull." Mr. Harding stared out into the night. "What I do know is that it was an accident, and that Charles went to his death without ever understanding how it could have happened."

"It's my mother's fault."

"Perhaps so."

But she was mine to blame—mine, not his. "And you?" I said rudely. "Did she hurl herself at you as well?"

He looked up. "What?"

"Down at the summerhouse? I heard you with her. You were saying, 'I've warned you, didn't I warn you——'"

All at once he was standing over me, towering over me. "Now you listen to me," he bellowed. "What I say or do not say to anyone, your mother included, is none of your damned business! How *dare* you tax me with it? How *DARE* you!"

I stared up at him, my heart beating in my neck.

"You want to know what I was warning her about? No, of course you don't. You've worked it out long since, haven't you? Creeping around, spying on other people's conversations! Unworthy, Cressida! This is entirely unworthy of you!"

I sank my head and covered my ears, but he just shouted on more loudly.

"You didn't think a man who looks like this could be

anything to a woman, did you? No, no, of course you didn't. You're too young, perhaps, to understand the power of money to overcome revulsion. Even Mrs. Arbuthnot was not without her ambitions in that direction. Ha!"

I looked up at him, tears streaming down my face.

"And do stop that sniveling. Pull yourself together. You're not a child anymore."

I started to stand. "May I please be excused?"

"*No you may not!* Sit down!"

I sat, but I would not look at him. I took out my hanky and blew my nose noisily.

He went to sit back down and was quiet for a long time before he said, "I asked you once what you dreamed of for your future. Do you remember that?"

I nodded.

"Any nearer? No? Well, what about the terrors? Still waking in the night?"

I looked up quickly.

"Your mother told me. She was concerned, and so am I."

But it was unbearable that they had me between them like a secret. "She's only concerned about herself!" I shouted. "And anyway, it's none of her business what happens here!"

"And none of mine, too, I suppose?" His face began to twist. "Cressida, Cressida! She only told me so that you wouldn't alarm me if you woke up. That is why I put you in Mrs. Arbuthnot's room in the first place. My mother is deaf as you know, and I wanted you within earshot. Tell me what it's all about."

"But I haven't had nightmares for years! She knows that! She's only trying to inveigle herself back in here with you!" I was on my feet now, hearing my voice rising and rising in the large room. "Anyway, I *never* had nightmares before we moved up here! Miranda was the one who had them! And we'd never have come here in the first place if my mother hadn't had ambitions like Mrs. Arbuthnot!"

"Ah," he sighed. "There you might be right."

But I didn't want to be right. I kept turning this way and that way as if I was looking for something to throw. "She's a trollop! She's a cheap bit of fluff like that mask you made me put on! So why do you even listen to her?"

He raised his eyebrow at this and opened his mouth to say something, but I went on before he could. "And how dare you spy on me? You have no right to spy on me even if it is your own house!"

"Spy?"

"Listening for nightmares! Checking up on everything I do! If my father were alive, I'd tell him what it's like here! I'd tell him you have a mistress up the coast, too! I've never wished for anything in my whole life as much as I wish he were alive!"

He clutched at the arms of the chair, rising out of it at last. "Cressida!"

But I ran past him and out of the room, through the hall and up the stairs. I slammed my door and would have locked it if there'd been a key. I stood in the middle of the room, in the dark, listening for his footsteps, wondering what would happen to me now.

Chapter 23

I wasn't much of a sulker, but I sulked for the next few evenings anyway. When dinner was over, I would make an excuse and go up to my room. From the side balcony I could see across the lawn, right into the old servants' quarters. Usually a light was on in there, and often Edgar's tutor would be standing at the corner window in his vest, just staring out into the darkness with his arms folded. He was a small, pale man with a round face and spectacles, and he taught at Boys' Prep in the mornings.

I switched on the balcony light and went out there in my shorty pajamas, as if I needed air. Perhaps he saw me, because, the next thing, his light went off. And, after that, it became a sort of game night after night—lights on, lights off, and when I met him at the gate in the mornings, he'd just hold it open, not even looking me in the eye.

And then, one evening, Mr. Harding looked up and said, "I'll tell you what I've been thinking. I've been thinking that

I'll ask your mother if I might hire away that driver of hers as a sort of housekeeper pro tem."

"Phineas?"

"I don't need a full-time driver, and Phineas could serve both functions quite easily. He might be glad of the chance, who knows?"

"How can Phineas be a housekeeper when he isn't a house-keeper?" I said, hearing my voice rising. Phineas spying on me would be even worse than Mr. Harding.

But the more anxious I became, the more he just sat back and smiled. "He kept your house very nicely, didn't he? To my mind, he kept it better than Mrs. Arbuthnot kept mine. Anyway, what I need right now is someone to run the kitchen properly and to supervise the cleaning of the house. My mother seems quite content to have the house girl ministering to her and you reading to her in the evenings. And who knows how long it would take for me to find someone other than you whom I could bear to have in my company."

I flushed at the compliment, I couldn't help it.

"My dear," he said. "I thought the idea would please you. I was sure it would."

The words and the softness of his voice had made my face and neck and ears flush even hotter, but with shame this time. Anyone could tell him how I paraded for the tutor on the balcony, any servant walking to the back gate would have only to look up and see me there. Even Edgar could look up on his way in or out. So why hadn't I thought of that before? What madness had me forgetting to consider the consequences of anything, even of landing back down the hill with Ma and Mr. Ledson?

I only saw Ma now when I went to Miranda's for tea on Sundays, after tennis. She'd become sallow and bony, and had a new creeping way of asking questions about Harding's Rest, which I pretended not to hear. And if I couldn't pretend, if I *had* to hear her say I should try teasing my hair or using a little eyeliner, I just tossed my head as if I knew better. Which, in fact, I did.

It was Mr. Harding who had suggested I grow my hair and wear it back in a chignon. "Fluffing it up into one of those bird's nests is common," he said. "And you are not to be common, Cressida." And so, as soon as it was long enough, I parted it in the middle and pulled it into a bun like a ballet dancer's. I even felt like a ballet dancer, taller and slimmer now, with the bones of my hips showing, and my breasts lovely and round. I would open both wardrobe doors to look at myself front and back, and then out I'd go onto the balcony so that the tutor could see me as well.

*

When I got to my room that night, I didn't switch on my light. I took my clothes off and felt my way across the room in the dark and out onto the balcony. There it was, the light of my old room floating in the darkness, and the tutor at the window, waiting for me. I leaned over the balustrade and stared back at him, naked, invisible, thinking how little difference it would make which stranger was over there, because all I wanted was to be seen before it was too late. Before I was old and sallow and worn out like Ma.

But just as I was standing up to switch on the light, the Beethoven romance started up downstairs. Mr. Harding must have opened the French doors to the garden so that I'd hear it too. Usually he went back to his study when I came upstairs. But perhaps he wanted me to come downstairs again tonight. Or perhaps he knew about the tutor and wanted to stop me before he had to send me home. You never knew with Mr. Harding until he'd made his mind up, and then it was too late.

I took my hairpins out and let my hair fall to my shoulders. The crickets were singing, they were almost as loud as the music, and there were mosquitoes whining around my head. They'd follow me inside and keep me awake all night, but I didn't care. If Mr. Harding was going to send me home, I'd be as common as I liked, even if it was only to stand in the dark on the balcony, naked, invisible.

Chapter 24

And then, one day as I climbed onto the bus to go home from my piano lesson, there was the tutor, blinking at me through his glasses. His small, neat fingers were clutching a satchel, and for a while we just looked away from each other. But then the bus began to fill up and he gave up his seat, and so did I. And so we were standing together, swaying and lurching against each other until we reached our stop.

"Going up the hill?" he said when we got off. So he was Scottish, which I might have known from his socks and sandals and the way he slung the satchel over one shoulder like a schoolboy. "I believe you used to have my job," he said with a smile as we turned the corner onto Montpelier.

I nodded, staring ahead at the carpet of jacaranda.

"You must be coming up for matric yourself this year? If you want any help with Latin or maths, those are my subjects. Going upcountry for the long weekend with the others?"

I stopped. "Upcountry?"

"Ay. So you're not going yourself then? Good, good."

*

All through dinner I waited for Mr. Harding to bring up the subject of the long weekend, and when he didn't, I said, "I think I'll start swotting for matric during the long weekend."

He banged out his pipe in the ashtray. "Changing your mind about university?"

"Do I have a choice?"

He gave out one of his barking laughs. "No, you do not! What about that Frank girl? Surely she's going?"

"She wants to go to Oxford."

"Oxford, hey?" He looked keen. "Well, what about you? What about Cambridge? That would certainly have pleased your papa."

I stared down at my hands. I was sick of the way he used my father to get what he wanted, sick of the way I couldn't say anything without him snatching it away for himself. Every month he left an envelope on the front kist for me as usual. It was much too much just for reading to old Mrs. Harding, I knew that, but I also knew that I was to buy my books and uniforms with it, and to use what was left over for pocket money. Since I'd moved up the hill, I'd never asked Ma for anything, although she was always offering me money when Miranda's back was turned.

"There's a whole set of exams to take," I said. "She has a special tutor, she and Maya Chowdree."

"Chowdree?" He leaned forward. "Vidi's daughter? I know Vidi well, I'll speak to him. No? Why not? You'd surely form a fine trio? Well, all right, if you're dead set against it, I have a tutor right here on the premises. No doubt you'd be a happy relief to him after Edgar. In fact, you can get started over the next few days. I'll be going inland for the long weekend, and I'm taking Edgar with me. My mother has chosen to remain here with you."

So I was a servant after all, left to look after an old woman whenever he felt like going away. And now I'd have the tutor to deal with as well.

"The staff will be here, of course," he said. "And Phineas. He's starting on the first of the month."

"Phineas?" It was getting worse and worse.

"Oh yes, all arranged. How far are you with the Galsworthy?"

I shrugged. I was sick of the Forsytes, too. I could hardly get through three sentences before Mrs. Harding would hold up her hand and say, "Stop! Could you read that funny bit again?"

"How are you doing with the Churchill?" he went on.

"I've finished *The Gathering Storm*."

"Ah! Then move on to *The Finest Hour* if you like. What did you think?"

"I think I've had enough of Churchill for the moment. Anyway, we're not even doing the First World War for matric. The history teacher says it's still controversial."

"Indeed?" he said airily. "Where shall we move on to then? My study is at your command." Everything he said now was like this, as if he didn't really care what I knew or didn't know anymore, even about the war. "Meanwhile, I'll make enquiries about these Oxford entrance exams and you should, too."

"When do you leave?" I asked. A dull weight had taken hold of my breathing.

He sat forward. "You'll be all right on your own here,

won't you? Probably be a nice break from my catechising you every chance I get. Ha!"

*

That night, for the first time since I'd come back to Harding's Rest, the Germans returned. They were in our old house this time, stamping through it, turning things over, tearing them up as they searched for me. I was hiding under the swing seat, and Mr. Harding saw me there, he was one of them, and just as they came out onto the verandah, I woke up screaming, trying to get out of the bed on the wrong side. I stood up and groped my way to the door, but just as I turned down the passage, there he was, a tall, dark shape against the light, and I screamed again.

"Cressida!" he said, rushing up. He was wearing a dressing gown, and his hair was sticking up all over his head. "What's the matter? I heard you from all the way down the passage."

I stood stiff in terror, still half in, half out of the dream. When he held out his hand I shrank from it and backed against the wall.

"Cressida," he said softly, coming to take me by the shoulders. "It's me, George Harding. Come, my dear." Switching on each light as we passed it, he led me along the passage and through the door to his wing. "Here," he said, opening a door into a small lounge. An electric fire was burning in there, and the dogs were spread out, asleep. He took a mohair rug from the couch and wrapped it around my shoulders. But still I was shivering, and when I sat down it was on the edge of the couch, ready to run if I had to.

Chapter 25

All the way upcountry I stared out of the car window, sullen with embarrassment. This was worse, far worse, than not being invited in the first place. I didn't belong there, I knew that. Everyone must have known, too, especially Mr. Harding. Upcountry was where the boarders at school came from, people who rode in gymkhanas and drew horses all over their books, and Ruth and I said they looked like horses themselves.

Mrs. Bourne-Thomas came out to meet us. She was pale and plain and certainly horsey. "Mrs. Harding!" she cried in a looping voice. "George! Edgar! And this must be Cressida! How glad I am that you could join us!" She put an arm around old Mrs. Harding and another through mine. "I often used to see your mother when I went to town," she said. "How is she doing these days?"

"Fine," I mumbled. "She's fine." Mrs. Bourne-Thomas was just the sort of upcountry woman Ma had taken to laughing at, now that she no longer had to serve her in a shop. "Pure jolly hockey sticks!" she'd say. "Pure jolly-haw-haw-cake-stand-at-the-bring-and-buy-sale!"

"Come in, let's have some tea," said Mrs. Bourne-Thomas. "I'll send the boy out for the luggage." She led us around the house and onto a deep, sprawling verandah. It was more like a room, really, than a verandah because there were walls at either end and couches and chairs, Persian rugs, a lovely old sideboard, and prints on the walls. The whole place smelled of thatch and floor polish and roses. There were bowls of them everywhere, lush and beautiful.

Mrs. Bourne-Thomas pulled a dog off the couch and settled herself in the corner, smiling at Mr. Harding. "So lovely to have you here again, George!" she said. "I thought I'd never lure you out of your castle."

He sat back in his chair, and even though he was wearing his hat and veil, I could see the way he was smiling back at her, the way he listened as she told him she was thinking of selling up and moving into town at the end of the year.

"Now that Nigel's gone," she said brightly, "there really is no point in staying out here anymore." She took a cigarette out of a silver case, and he held her hand steady while he lit it for her.

"I'll wait for Guy to finish school, of course," she said. "He's beginning to panic, I'm happy to say."

Mr. Harding turned to me. "So is Cressida, although she'd have me believe she wants nothing to do with a university."

She laughed. "Poor things!" she said. "I still remember how awful it all was, don't you? By the way, how goes that book?"

"Never going be finished, I'm afraid. I undo today what I did up yesterday. I'm beginning to think that's the point of the enterprise."

"Keeping the suitors at bay?" Again the laugh.

I looked out over the garden, homesick suddenly for every-thing I'd left behind at Harding's Rest, even Churchill.

"Guy wants to go to the Continent at the end of the year," she said. "He's got it into his head that he's going into archi-tecture. But we shall see, we shall see."

"Guy?" said old Mrs. Harding suddenly. "Who's Guy?"

"Guy Bourne-Thomas, my son. I don't think you've met him yet, Mrs. Harding. He should be here in time for dinner. He's on the afternoon train."

"Bourne-Thomas? Bourne-Thomas? Didn't we know a Bourne-Thomas once, Charles?"

"Indeed we did, Mother. Nigel. He was at school with Charles. I'm afraid he died a few months ago."

"Nigel Bourne-Thomas!" old Mrs. Harding cried. "Used to wet the bed! We were always having to put a rubber sheet down when he came for the weekend."

Mrs. Bourne-Thomas broke into her looping laugh. "Oh, Mrs. Harding!" she cried. "I wish you'd told me that before he got away! I could have had a field day with that!"

"May I go to the station to meet Guy?" Edgar asked quickly. He was sitting with his legs crossed like Mr. Hard-ing's, thigh over thigh, looking almost normal in his khaki slacks and white open-necked shirt.

"Well, of course!" said Mrs. Bourne-Thomas. "He'll be expecting you. I already told the driver."

"Charles," old Mrs. Harding said, pushing herself up, "I'm ready to go home whenever you are."

"Oh, Mrs. Harding!" Mrs. Bourne-Thomas jumped up. "We're so hoping you'll stay for the weekend. May I show you up to your room? I do hope you'll like it. It looks right out over the garden, you know, right down to the river. See the weeping willows? The river's down there."

"Shall I go up?" I said quickly. "I brought a book to read to Mrs. Harding."

"Oh no!" sang Mrs. Bourne-Thomas. "You stay here and enjoy your tea."

But I wanted to go. It would have made me feel less stupid for being there at all. When Mr. Harding had taken me back to my room after the nightmare, he'd glanced around at the snapshots of my father on the wall, picked up the framed photograph next to my bed, and stared at it for a long time, saying nothing. Then he'd taken my hand and said, "Pack a suitcase tomorrow, you're coming upcountry with me."

"I should go," I whispered to him now. "Mrs. Harding is used to me."

"Cressida," he said low and sharp, "do try to enjoy yourself, won't you? Why don't you and Edgar take a stroll down to the river when you've finished your tea? It's the perfect time of day, before the mist starts rolling in."

*

"They sent us down here to get rid of us," I said. "Like children." I clasped my arms around my knees and stared at the river.

"Don't put your feet in the water," Edgar said. "There's bilharzia."

"Is Mrs. Bourne-Thomas his mistress?"

"What?"

"Mr.—Harding's—Mistress. Everyone knows he has one."

"Rot! That's rot!"

I sighed and lay back on the bank. "You said you hated

everyone at Somerset. Do you hate Guy, too?" It was the first time I'd ever mentioned anything from that day in the summerhouse, and I looked up to see what he'd do about it.

But he just grabbed a willow branch and began to stroke it as if it were a dog. "Not Guy," he said. "Guy's decent."

"Do you also want to be an architect?" It was impossible to imagine Edgar wanting to do anything but hang around aimlessly, failing at everything he did.

He shook his head.

"What then?"

"He'll never let me anyway, so what's the point?"

"Let you what?" I sat up. *"What?"*

"Go to the Tech."

"The Tech? You want to be a hairdresser?"

"No!"

"What then?"

He turned to me desperately. "Don't say anything. If you do, I'll just say I never said it."

"Don't be stupid!" But a wave of happiness was flushing through me at the thought of Mr. Harding's face when he found out about the Tech. "When are you going to tell him?"

But he was scrambling away from me, up the bank. And so I lay back on the grass, listening to the river. There were only three nights to get through here, only nine months left of school. And if Mrs. Bourne-Thomas came to live in town after I'd left, why should I even care?

*

When I came in, I found old Mrs. Harding clacking her false teeth at Mrs. Bourne-Thomas.

"Ah, Cressida, there you are!" said Mr. Harding. "Would

you mind retrieving *The Forsyte Saga* after all? Perhaps Mrs. Bourne-Thomas would be so kind as to send some supper up to my mother's room, and you'd read to her as usual?"

"Nonsense!" cried Mrs. Bourne-Thomas. "Cressida will want to freshen up before the young people come back from the station. Take my advice, my dear," she said to me. "Go and have a nice bath before the boys hog all the hot water. Let's all go up together, shall we? I'll show you your room, and you'll give me the book."

*

When I came down, Guy was there, tangled up on the floor with the dogs. He was tall and thin and pale like Mrs. Bourne-Thomas, and when he scrambled to his feet, he was blushing as furiously as Edgar, which made it easier to shake the hand he held out, and to ask how long the train took from Somerset.

Mr. Harding sat on the couch, watching us through his veil. Mrs. Bourne-Thomas was watching, too, sliding her eyes towards me whenever she thought I wasn't looking. She was wearing a tweed skirt and a light blue twinset now, and her hair was clipped back with a tortoiseshell grip like a schoolgirl's. "Guy," she said, "are you riding tomorrow?"

Guy laughed. "Probably not, Mater. I want to sleep late."

"And you, Cressida?" she said.

"I'm dead scared of horses, I'm afraid," I said, trying for a casual smile. But it must have sounded like a request because, the next thing, there was Guy, offering to teach me.

"Oh no, no thank you!" I said quickly, staring down at my lap with my ears flaming. Sitting there, ridiculous in Ma's black velvet dress, I had no proper voice for these people, no proper anything. I often wore the dress to dinner with Mr. Harding and never felt ridiculous there, even though it was really a dance dress, with a low lace neckline and a wide gathered skirt. When Ma had worn it, she'd put on her high-heeled silver sandals and her ankle bracelet as well.

Mrs. Bourne-Thomas kicked off her shoes and tucked her stockinged feet under her. Nothing she did or wore or said could ever be common, I could see that. And Mr. Harding was at home with her as he'd never been with us. He smiled, he joked, he said he'd have a look at Nigel's old MG to see if it was worth resuscitating, and would she like to stay at Harding's Rest while she looked for a house in town? She'd be doing him a favour, he said, the place was like a morgue, a whole wing of it virtually uninhabited.

By the time we were back on the verandah after dinner, he was asking Mrs. Bourne-Thomas if she'd keep an eye out for a housekeeper, too. The last one had lost him a few servants, he said, and a considerable portion of his mother's sanity.

She laughed. "Oh dear! How are you coping in the meanwhile?"

"I have a competent African holding the fort, and Cressida is doing yeoman's service with my mother. However," he said, looking at me, "she's going to be abandoning Edgar and me in a few months for greater things, and we'll have to look elsewhere for company."

"What nonsense!" said Mrs. Bourne-Thomas, waving him away. "If you wanted company you'd have gathered some in long ago."

"Help me on this one, please, Cressida," he said. "Am I not the very essence of congeniality?"

I tried to join in, but I could hardly breathe. My black velvet had been ridiculous at Harding's Rest, too, I could see that now. All Ma's dresses were ridiculous, they were as ridiculous as she was, and I couldn't wait to take my money out of the building society and buy myself a tweed skirt and twinset. Even Edgar belonged here more than I did. There he was, sitting out on the steps with Guy, talking away as if he were a normal person.

Perhaps Mrs. Bourne-Thomas saw all this, too, because she leaned towards me and said, "By the way, isn't it absolutely marvelous, what your sister's made of the Cotton Reel? Such a *gorgeous* little boutique it is now! All the upcountry women I know make a beeline for it whenever they go to town."

There was no answering this. Everyone knew Miranda was as common as dust—fat and common and cheap. As far as Mrs. Bourne-Thomas was concerned, I was probably common as dust myself, sitting there, dark and awkward and silent. To her I must have looked like just another of Mr. Harding's eccentric projects. After all, he'd never been quite the same since he'd come back from the war, had he? He'd been too much alone, everyone said so—shut off like that with a dippy old mother, an illegitimate nephew, and now a seventeen-year-old girl of questionable background.

Chapter 26

As far as Mrs. Bourne-Thomas knew, we left after breakfast the next morning because old Mrs. Harding had been fussing all through the night. But really it was because I had woken up screaming again, and Mr. Harding, who was in the room next door, had come running in. He'd been listening for me, he said, worrying about me all day.

"Where's the switch?" he said, feeling along the wall. "Where's the bloody switch?"

But, before I could tell him, he gave up and strode across the room. "Cressida?" he said, looming over the bed. He took me by the shoulders and gave me a shake. "Wake up! Are you fully awake?"

He sat on the edge of the bed, staring down at me. The moon, shining in through the voiles, caught the mirror on the wardrobe and in its strange reflection he was more terrifying than ever. "You're going to tell me what this is all about," he said in a low echoing voice. "What is it that wakes you up like this? *Tell* me!"

"It's stupid."

"Perhaps so. But you're going to tell me anyway." He took me hard by the chin and turned my face to his. "Now!"

Suddenly there were no reasons I could give him, only blame. "It's *your* fault," I said. "It's always been your fault. Miranda's nightmares, and mine as well."

He stiffened at this, but he let go of my chin.

"Always wanting us to know how lucky we were! Giving my mother those concentration-camp books! If it wasn't for you we'd never even have *known* what the Germans did!"

He sighed. "Cressida, I cannot condone ignorance, certainly not on that score."

"But you wouldn't have given those books to Mrs. Bourne-Thomas, would you?" I was almost shouting now. "You wouldn't have forced *her* to know what could have happened!"

For a while all I could hear was the rasp of his breathing. And then, at last, he said, "Elspeth Bourne-Thomas has nothing to do with this."

"So?" I shouted, furious tears storming down my cheeks. "So what? You don't take your hat off in front of *her*, but you took it off for us! You didn't care how *we'd* feel!"

"Cressida, Cressida!" He reached forward and lifted me up, out of the eiderdown, folding his arms so tightly around me that I could feel his heart thumping against my shoulder. "You are right, you are right about everything. But didn't I try to warn you all those years ago? Didn't I try?"

And then suddenly, before I could tell him that really I didn't care about the hat or the books, that I didn't blame him for anything, he'd pushed me away and leaped to his feet. And when I reached up and grabbed on to his dressing gown to

pull him back, he just unwound my fingers and walked quickly
out of the room, closing the door behind him.

I jumped out of bed to follow him. But suddenly, standing
there, shivering in my nightie and bare feet, it was as if I were
in the middle of the sea, and everywhere I looked was impossible. And yet nothing was ever impossible for him. I could hear
him out there now, making his way down the passage.

*

He didn't look up when I came in. He was sitting in an armchair, his chin resting on his hands. So I just stood where I
was, listening to the creaking of the thatch. And then I said,
"It was my mother you tried to warn, not me."

I heard the words dropping and dropping into the silence
between us. It was cold. All the windows were open and mosquitoes were whining around my head.

"Oh Christ!" he said, jumping suddenly to his feet and
coming over to me. He took my face in both hands. Then he
ran his fingers around my jaw, my ears, my neck, but so lightly,
like a blind man, that I thought if I moved it might never have
happened.

"You're cold," he whispered. I could smell the cognac on
his breath, and his soap, and the sweet smell of the thatch,
dark and wonderful. "Come on," he said, taking me by the
hand to lead me out again as if I were a child.

But I pulled my hand back. "Wait!" I said, grabbing at
my nightie and flinging it away. I flung my hair back, too, so
that he could see everything naked, even my face. I stared at
him. Outside there was the rush of the river, the crickets singing as if everything were normal. But it wasn't. There he was,
a dark, silent shape against the windows, and it was just as
well I couldn't see his face because the sight of him staring

back could have made it seem ridiculous, which it probably was anyway.

And so really he would have been right to warn me after all, because I was the one who went up to him now, before he could tell me not to. I was the one who locked my hands around his neck and stood shivering against him. And for a few moments it was as if I'd taken hold of a ghost, and if I let go, he might vanish, back to what he'd been before.

Chapter 27

Spero meliora. All the way home I'd stared out of the car window, wanting nothing more than for the night to come. And then, when we arrived, and Phineas came out to fetch the luggage, Mr. Harding told him he'd have his lunch on a tray in his study, and didn't even turn around to glance at me.

I stared after him. "Don't trust this happiness," he'd said the night before. "Believe me, Cressida, it's a trick, a momentary reprieve, that's all." And I'd run a finger along the scars on his chin as if I'd never dreaded the touch of them, the touch of him either. There were scars everywhere, up and down his side. "Can you feel this?" I'd said. "And this?" And then he'd put a hand over mine and said, "This is not at all what I have in mind for you." So I'd laughed. "I'm tired of what you have in your mind for me," I'd said.

And he'd laughed, too, and pulled me back to him. "Ah Cressida," he'd said with a sigh. "*Spero meliora.* That must be your motto."

Ruth's cousin had told her it was like being lifted up and carried along, that there was nothing you could do about it, no matter what you knew of the consequences. But it had been nothing like that with Mr. Harding. All the time he'd been looming and heaving over me, asking again and again if he was hurting me, I'd just stared up into the darkness, wondering what would happen now, when we got back to Harding's Rest. And then, when it was over at last and he was lying next to me, saying, "I might have known it would come to this; it's like the terror of death, felt long before one has the words to understand it"—that's when I stopped wondering completely, stopped listening, too, because I might have known all along myself that this was what I wanted—to have Mr. Harding next to me like that, stroking me, talking to me as I lay naked, triumphant, free.

*

Downstairs the tea tray was rattling through to the verandah as if nothing had changed. And, for all I knew, nothing really had. When Phineas came knocking, as usual to say tea was ready, the old madam was waiting, I told him I had a headache and was going to lie down.

So there I lay like a fool, listening for the creak of Mr. Harding on the stairs, and when he didn't come to my door, I ran a bath and sat in it until it was cold. And really, he might as well have been a ghost after all, and the whole thing a trick, except that to him I was probably just a cheap tart now like Miranda, except that even she must have been lifted up and carried along, or why would she have let it ruin her life in the first place?

*

I waited all through dinner for Mr. Harding to look up. But he just pushed his lamb chop around on the plate without even eating it.

"Cressida," he said at last, putting his knife and fork together, "if you'd still like my help preparing for exams, we can carry on as before. You'll come to my study after tea——" He stopped, and shook his head, and put his hand to his forehead. "Oh, for God's sake, Cressida, I'm asking you for the impossible. But the alternative is worse. I'd have to send you away, and I cannot bear to do that."

"*Away?* Where to?" I jumped up, knocking over my wineglass.

"Leave it! Leave it!" He was standing now too. "I don't know, really I cannot think at the moment."

"I don't *care* about last night!" Tears were storming down my face now. "It wasn't even your fault! You never asked me to come to your room in the first place!"

"I'd been asking you for years, you little fool, if only you'd been able to see it."

I stared at him. "How? When?"

But he just rang the bell. "No pudding tonight," he said to Phineas. "Bring the coffee to the lounge, and then you can all leave."

*

We sat in silence with our coffee.

Then he said, "All day I've been thinking about those nightmares of yours—no, don't worry, I'm not going to start that up again. What I've been thinking is how curiously appropriate they are."

I waited. I was used to the way he'd latch on to a subject, no matter what was going on around it.

"Until last night it had never occurred to me that the horror could come alive for someone who hadn't been born until it was over—brought back into existence, if you will, by my own misplaced pedantry. That, and the horror of my own face and head. Ha!"

I flushed. I opened my mouth to say something, anything to take it all back. But he held up his hand.

"No! Please! It doesn't suit you to be superficial." He began to light his cigar, turning his good side to me as usual. "When I told you I'd moved to the north wing because I wanted privacy, that wasn't entirely true. The fact is, I suffered nightmares myself and they were alarming my mother. Cognac?" He went over to the drinks tray and poured us each a glass.

"You cannot see what I saw and come out intact," he said. "And that's only to consider what I *saw*, safe on the other side of the fence. How much worse, as you quite rightly surmise in your nightmares, to have been a victim oneself. Even a potential victim."

I nodded, but really all I wanted now was for him to come over and take me by the shoulders again.

"'Surmise' isn't even the word," he went on. "But there aren't any words for it really. Words are impotent in the face of such a thing, don't you see? They're irrelevant. They can't come anywhere near the depth and length and breadth of it."

I swallowed my cognac in one gulp just as he'd always told me not to. The dogs were scratching to be let in and I longed to ask if it would be superficial of me to get up and open the

door. Usually I could joke with him like that, but now everything was different.

He stood up. "Go to bed now," he said. His voice was soft,
and I wondered if this was the sort of invitation I'd never been
able to see before. But it was impossible to ask. Once you had
to ask, you'd never find out. It was like considering the consequences of something before you actually did it. Doomed to
failure right from the start.

Part Three

Chapter 28

I had to leave Harding's Rest anyway because Mr. Ledson decided to give up on Ma after all, and now that she had the house to herself again, she saw no reason for me to impose upon George Harding any further. It was going to be like old times, she said, we were even getting our old furniture back, thanks to Mr. Harding. Everything, in fact, was thanks to Mr. Harding again. If he hadn't called in his lawyers, Ledson would have left Ma with nothing, not even the shop. And all Mr. Harding was asking in return was that I go up to the big house for tea every weekday afternoon. Old Mrs. Harding had grown fond of me, he'd told her, and he himself wished to continue preparing me for my exams.

I stared around my old room, breathing so lightly that I had to sit down on my suitcase. It had all happened so quickly that even though I knew one thing had nothing to do with the other, it was as if I were the one being punished by everyone.

Ma put her hands on my shoulders. "See how I had the basin taken out? Who needs a basin in a room anymore? I put the old wicker chair in that corner, see? Somehow it makes the room look bigger, don't you think?"

There was something imploring about her now that made me want to shake her off. "It's ridiculous!" I spat out, jumping to my feet. "Every time something goes wrong in your life I'm the one who has to pay for it!"

I picked up my suitcase and swung it onto the bed. "Here," I said, pulling out all the clothes she'd given me. "I won't need these anymore."

"Really?" She picked them up one by one and then folded them carefully into a pile. She was losing her beauty, everything about her seemed to be loosening and softening and drying up, even her hair. It was dead black now, I'd seen the bottle of dye in the bathroom.

"The thing is, Ma," I said more gently, "I want some things of my own. I have some money saved up. Mr. Harding still pays me, I don't know why."

She brightened immediately. "Well, I'm at loose ends tomorrow. Want to go to town?" She held up the black velvet. "Are you sure about this one? It's Jonathan Logan, you know, and that collar is guipure lace! You looked so lovely in it at Giant's Peak."

It was the first time she'd mentioned Giant's Peak since New Year's Eve. "I think I'll go to town on my own, if you don't mind," I said.

"Oh, don't be silly! If you go on your own you'll be treated like a schoolgirl. And you'll never be able to get them to bring out what they keep behind."

*

I didn't even need to try on the shirtwaister to know that it was perfect. But I took it into the dressing room anyway. I turned up the collar, plunged my hands into the pockets, stood on my toes, and twirled this way and that way. A great lightness had suddenly taken hold of my heart, lifting it, floating it free. For weeks it had sat like a stone in my chest, weighing everything down. But now, in that moment, there seemed to be a future to look forward to, something far beyond Oxford, and school, and Ma, and even Mr. Harding himself.

"I didn't want to say anything in front of her," Ma whispered as we came out of Better Dresses, "but don't you think that was a *ridiculous* price to pay for a cotton frock? Even if it is imported?"

I shrugged. The shirtwaister had used up almost a quarter of my money, but buying it only infected me with a great greed for more. "I'm going up to look for a straight skirt and a twin-set now," I said. "I can easily take the bus home if you like."

She followed me in silence, pretending not to notice what I was choosing or spending. But then, as soon as we were in the car again, she said bitterly, "He must be overpaying you ridiculously for the little bit you do up there."

I turned to look out at the Saturday shoppers swarming to the bus stop. It was lovely, after all, to have her jealous again, and all my new things to look forward to. "Mr. Harding doesn't like me to look cheap," I said.

"Doesn't he, indeed? Well, I'm glad he's the one footing the bill because I certainly wouldn't!" She gripped the wheel furiously, surging and lurching with the traffic. She'd always driven like this, as if she couldn't think five feet in front of her. "Look," she said after a while, "there's something I feel I should warn you about."

"I've still got some money, don't worry."

"Not the money, that's your business. It's George Harding. If you're conceiving any romantic notions about him, you'd better think again."

"*What?*" We were coming out of town now, starting up the hill.

"Whatever you may think, he's a man after all, regardless of his afflictions. Rather an appealing one, some women might say. So if you think he's sitting up there waiting for your visits, you'd be quite mistaken."

"Oh, *please!*"

"Well, I'm just trying to warn you, that's all. You're not a baby anymore, and you should be aware that he's a man. A real man."

But it was unbearable—the words in her mouth, the sound and the sense of them. "*I don't want to hear!*" I shouted.

We were turning into the driveway, and she pressed the hooter for Elias. "By the way," she said, "you might feel Mr. Harding out about Phineas when you go up on Monday. Now that things are back to normal here, I'd like to have him back, too. After all, I'm the one who took him on raw from the kraal. You might find a nice way of pointing that out."

I jumped out of the car and slammed the door hard. "You can do your own feeling out and pointing out! Why not take *The Odyssey* and go down to his summerhouse again? It's always worth a try!"

She slammed her own door, too, back to herself at last. "Selfish!" she shouted. "You've always been selfish! And if you think I'm going to pin your hems for you, you've got another think coming!"

Chapter 29

We'd already gone through our class for the day—Edict of Nantes: Causes and Consequences, The War of the Roses: When and Why?—and I, half bored, half faint from the smell of his pipe and the sound of his voice, had gabbled out the answers. "Good," he'd said. "Now compare 'Ode on a Grecian Urn' with 'Ozymandias.'"

"Tomorrow," he said, "I'd like you to go across to Campbell. He's better equipped than I in Latin and maths. Shall we say Tuesdays and Fridays to him? The rest for me?"

"I don't see why I need him," I said quickly. "I'm top of the class in maths and second in Latin."

"Pride?" He twisted his face into one of his sarcastic smiles. "Proverbs 16. Recite!"

"I'm sick of pretending that nothing has changed," I said. "I may be proud, but you are dishonourable."

All the way up the hill I'd been practicing the word, wondering how to slip it in so that it would hit him like a stone.

"Dishonourable?" He threw his head back in a roaring laugh. "Oh, Cressida, what have you been reading to have come up with such a line?"

I stared into his twisted smile.

"The alternative would be not to see you at all, and I'm not sure I could bear that," he said lightly. It was the voice I heard, deep and soft, as I translated Virgil or worked out a theorem, so that I couldn't tell anymore what I would know for myself without him.

I looked down at the book on my lap. The first time I'd come to this study, all there'd been to dread were Germans coming through the window, and all I'd wanted was to have our old house back, our old life with it.

"So," he said, "tomorrow to Campbell? I'll alert him that you're coming."

I'd met the tutor at the bus stop the week before, and he'd asked if I'd like to go to the pictures on Saturday afternoon. He'd blushed as he spoke, and then walked on before I could even finish saying no I couldn't, I had tennis every Saturday. And after that I'd forgotten about him completely.

"Phineas will take you back down the hill after you've read to my mother. I don't want you walking in the dark."

I stood up, taller than usual in my new cork wedges. "I was the one who was dishonourable," I said quickly, not wanting, even now, to let the word go. "I'd do it again except that that's an hypothesis that never quite works, does it?"

He laughed. "Ah, there's my Cressida! You've a new dress, I see, and it suits you very well. Come over here, let me have a look at you." He took my hand and held it to his lips, and if he was joking again I didn't care. "Does your mother still go to the Film Society?"

"My mother?" For two days I'd hardly spoken to her except to say yes or no.

"*Night and Fog* is playing on Saturday evening and I'd recommend your seeing it, nightmares notwithstanding."

"She doesn't go anymore. And I don't have nightmares either."

"Then perhaps you'd allow me to take you?" He looked at his watch. "We still have ten minutes. Sit down. I don't think I've ever told you how I really came by Edgar."

"Edgar?"

"And I'd like to tell you now. Before we see the film."

*

It had started with a boy he'd searched for long before he found Edgar. This boy had been born in an attic in Paris, where his mother was hiding from the Germans. But after a while the crying had made it dangerous for everyone, and so the concierge persuaded the mother to let her take the baby to her own mother in the country. And even there he wasn't safe, because how was the mother going to account for a dark, circumcised baby when the Germans came nosing around? So she handed him over to a peasant who had dark-haired children of his own, and was already hiding a wounded English airman.

One evening, when the peasant didn't come back from his fields, the airman bundled up the child and crept away into the night, tying a hanky over the child's mouth to muffle his crying. And that turned out to be the third miracle of the boy's life because soon after he had been taken to the country, his mother was discovered anyway, and sent off to Auschwitz, and the concierge was shot as an example to others. And the very evening the airman was stealing away, the peasant was being tortured by the Germans into confessing. But, by the time they reached the farmhouse, baby and airman were gone. So the Germans hanged the peasant from his own tree, leaving his body there to rot and fall to the ground. And all this the airman had only found out later.

Meanwhile, he'd found his way back to England, where he landed up in a hospital bed right next to Mr. Harding's. What had happened to the baby the airman never found out because, as soon as he was well enough to fly again, he was shot down over the Channel. At first it had felt like just another absence of war, Mr. Harding said. But then he'd begun to think about the baby, and somehow the boy's luck enchanted him because of what he himself had seen. So, as soon as the war was over, he set about trying to find the child, which was a devil of a business because the baby had been taken over to England after all, and put into an orphanage, and then adopted by a childless couple, who refused all requests to see him.

And so, at last, Mr. Harding had given up. And then, after he'd come home, he'd found Charles's bastard in the crèche and had had to content himself with that.

Chapter 30

All through the lesson the tutor's ears burned like electric coils. When he thought I wasn't noticing, he'd stare at me as I pored over my Caesar. "The thing is," he said, "they want the translation not only correct but also elegant. See here"—he ran a freckled finger along the exercise book—"'In the winter that followed, which was the year in which the Usipetes, of German stock, and also the Tencteri, etcetera'—that's awkwardly put, don't you see?"

It was hot, and there were large semicircles of damp on his shirt. When he lifted his arm to look at his watch I had to turn away from the smell of his raw sweat. "There's some cake for tea," he said. "They sent it over from the big house." And before I could say I'd had tea already, he was jumping up and walking through to the kitchen.

The place seemed empty, now that our furniture was gone. Nothing fitted, nothing matched. And when the tutor came in with the tray I saw that the tea things didn't match either. "Here," he said, going through to the lounge, "it's more comfortable over here."

"Want me to pour?" I said.

"Lots of milk for me, please. When I drink beer I drink beer." He gave a forced little laugh. "Look," he said, "it's probably easier if you call me Jock. My real name's Andrew, but no one calls me that."

I handed him his cup. So far I'd called him nothing, but "Jock" would be quite impossible.

"I know you're Cressida, of course. How did your parents come to give you the name?"

"My mother's idea of a joke, I suppose."

"Well, I think it's beautiful." He put his cup down on the saucer and looked at me. "I think you're beautiful, too."

There were servants talking at the back gate, and Edgar could come back from Delaney any minute. Mr. Harding would want to know what we'd covered during the lesson, and suddenly it all seemed impossible, even sitting there on that couch, wanting Campbell to touch me with his freckled fingers.

Just then a clock started striking and I jumped to my feet. "I have to go and read to Mrs. Harding," I said, grabbing up my things.

"Friday, then?"

"Yes. Yes."

*

On Friday we sat at the table again as if he'd never told me I was beautiful. And when the lesson was almost over and I thought he'd forgotten, suddenly his hand was on my hair, stroking it, winding a strand of it on his fingers as I tried to rule a line. I sat very still, the pencil frozen in my hand. Then he turned my head quickly to his and kissed me, breathing hard.

"Please," he said, pulling me up, leading me through to the lounge. "Please!" he whispered, his hands under my skirt, pulling at my bloomers. He took off his glasses with one hand, never letting me go. And then he pulled me down onto the couch, kissing me here and there, and somehow he'd got his trousers off, too, because there he was, I could feel him against me, pushing himself onto me, into me, rolling me over so that he was under me like a horse, grunting and heaving, and if anyone had come in, it wouldn't have made any difference because I'd forgotten about everyone, even him, and they could have killed me if they'd wanted to, I'd never have been able to stop, never, not until it was all over at last.

He stared at me for a long time. "Don't worry," he said, "I used a French letter."

The couch was narrow, one of my legs was hanging over the edge and my skirt was all around me like a parachute. "I have to go," I said.

He reached for me, trying to hold me back. "If you knew how I've been longing for you over all these months," he said.

But I did know, I did. And now it had happened, and with a French letter. The girls at school were always whispering about French letters, and Ruth said, Agh, can you imagine? We still walked home from school together, and once, on Mr. Harding's riding afternoon, she'd come in for tea. But then, as soon as tea was over and we'd gone down to the summer-house, there was Mr. Harding himself, standing on the upper terrace in his jodhpurs, and the hat and veil. "God, Cress!" she'd whispered, standing up to be introduced. "How can you bear it?"

I stood up, and found my bloomers, and pulled them on, trying not to see the tutor as he buttoned up his trousers. I hated him now, I loathed everything about him, and yet, stupid as it was, when he turned and grabbed me, kissing me hard on the mouth, it could have started all over again right then if I hadn't had to go to old Mrs. Harding and read her *The Forsyte Saga*.

Chapter 31

As soon as I was in the car and going back down the hill, the afternoon began to weigh on me more heavily than anything in my life. Even Phineas's silence felt like a judgment. "Phin," I said, "I wish you'd come back to us."

He said nothing. He'd never been able to talk and drive at the same time.

"I mean, even if you could just teach Elias? He's hopeless."

He turned into the driveway and pulled up the brake. "Madam she must teach him."

"That's rubbish! You know Ma can't cook!"

He laughed at last. "You still rude," he said. "Where your auntie? She coming home now too?"

"Ma," I said, bursting into the kitchen, "what's going to happen with Bunch now?"

She wiped an arm across her forehead. Her makeup was running and her hair was coming out of its clips.

"I mean, is she coming back?" Everywhere I turned now there was something to worry about.

"Bunch?" she said. "Paid up at Our Jewish Home through the end of the year. After that, unless a miracle occurs, I suppose I'll have to have her back."

She poked at the chopped herring and pulled a face. Miranda had joined the Reform shul. She was even hauling Derek in there for conversion classes every Tuesday and Thursday evenings. So now there had to be candles and kiddush on Friday nights, and Ma herself had had to climb up to the storage room to find my father's old candlesticks and kiddush cup, which had taken Elias half the afternoon to polish.

"It's ridiculous!" I said. "What does Miranda know about being Jewish?"

Every week Ruth's family had Friday night dinners. Before Giant's Peak, she'd invited me to two of them, and there'd been cousins and aunts and uncles, everyone knowing all about being Jewish.

"She says she remembers Friday nights from before your father's accident," Ma said.

"Well I don't. And if it weren't for Mr. Harding I wouldn't know the first thing about being Jewish either."

She looked up fiercely. "Mr. Harding this, Mr. Harding that! And look at you! You look as if you've been dragged through a bush backwards! Go and tidy up before they arrive."

I walked through to the hall and stared at myself in the mirror, touching my flushed cheeks, my wild hair. I could have stopped him, it would have been easy. But all I could think now was that he'd be waiting for me on Tuesday, and then again on Friday, and it didn't matter how much I hated him or what I decided not to do, I knew I'd be back on the couch with him anyway.

*

Miranda fingered the cotton of my shirtwaister. She was fatter and blonder than ever, buttoned tightly into a cotton knit dress and matching belt. She made her own clothes now, Ma said, her own patterns as well. "Ma told me you came home with a whole new wardrobe," she said.

"Drink anyone?" said Ma, coming through from the kitchen with the nuts.

"I'll have a brandy and ginger ale," said Miranda. "And Derek will have a Castle."

"Derek can fetch his own Castle if he can tear himself away from the cricket. Cressida? Want a drink?"

I shook my head.

"Hasn't George Harding introduced you to wine?"

"Wine?" said Miranda. "That's the least of it. You'd be surprised, the things I hear about George Harding."

"Without him," said Ma, "you'd be in the haberdashery department at Cottam's. *If* you were lucky."

Miranda shrugged. Ma's threats didn't seem to worry her anymore. Nothing seemed to worry her, not even her enormous stomach.

"You're not pregnant again, are you?" I said. Everything seemed to remind me of what I'd done, now that I knew how easy it could be.

Ma gave one of her hard laughs. "She'd better not be. I paid a fortune to have all that taken care of."

"Albert's the one who paid," said Miranda. "By the way, I saw the new wife. *She's* the one who's pregnant."

Ma tried a wave of the hand, but her face was livid and she had to sit down.

It was only half past six. There was still supper to endure, candles and kiddush and Miranda's boys screaming from room to room. "Come," I said to her, "I'll show you what I bought."

"Don't be long, girls!" Ma called after us. "Supper's almost on the table."

"She's just jealous," Miranda said as we walked down the passage to my room. She was wearing too much perfume, too much of everything.

I opened the wardrobe and brought out my new things, laid them on the spare bed. They looked measly there, ordinary, too, in the way the house looked ordinary now—an ordinary house with ordinary rooms, ordinary everything in it.

"Pringle?" she said, holding up the cardigan. "Golly!"

"Miranda," I said quickly, "are you ever sorry you met Derek? I mean so young?"

For a moment I thought she'd flash at me the way she'd flashed at Ma. But she didn't, she just slumped back into the wicker chair. "Sorry?" she said. "Sorry? I'm sorry every day of my life."

I began to put the clothes back in the wardrobe.

"Why do you ask?" she said. "Have you got a boyfriend?"

I shrugged.

"Well listen, you, be careful. And keep him away from Harding's Rest. Don't throw your luck away, now that you've got George Harding wound around your little finger."

"What?" I laughed. For the first time ever Miranda had actually given me hope. "Careful of what?"

"It's a trick, they trick you." She stood up and steadied herself on her high, high heels. "Don't believe what they tell you. Just remember me when they start trying their tricks on you."

Chapter 32

As soon as the lights went down at Film Society, Mr. Harding took off his hat and put it on the floor at his feet. But his head caught the light of the screen and I could see his jaw clenched tight, the furious, twisting stare. I tried to be furious myself, but as long as I had Campbell to worry about it was impossible. I stared at the rows of toilets with horrible stalactites around each hole, and the windows of the brothel, and the scratches on the gas chamber ceiling, but all I could think of was what I could say to get out of Tuesdays and Fridays.

Perhaps it would have been different if I'd gone to the film alone. But with Mr. Harding next to me it was as if I were seeing everything the way he must have seen it when he was there himself. And then it was back to Campbell—the clouds of hair between the women's legs, the men trying to cover themselves in front of the camera.

All around people were sighing, sniffing, shaking their

heads at the rolls of cloth made out of women's hair, the skin used as parchment to draw on. But even the Germans, standing about so pleased with themselves, made me think of the brothel they used, the girls lying on the beds inside.

It was only when the bulldozers began tumbling bodies into a pile that I remembered my father, and how Ma had wanted him to go off to war for her own sake. And just as I was managing to fall into a sort of glorious sorrow for him at last, the film was over and the lights went up, and there was Mr. Harding, putting a hand on my arm and saying, "Let's leave before the rush."

*

"Who really mourns?" he said, staring down into his glass of sangria. "Even twenty years on? Think of it. Twenty years, and who will mourn your loss? Who will mourn mine? I'll tell you—no one." He twisted around to me. "Those nightmares of yours, what are they really about? Pain? Death? Certainly. But most of all, obliteration. Your own. Singular."

We had the far corner table at the Matador. It was crowded with Film Society people as I'd known it would be, which was why I'd asked him to take me there. After all, what was the point of wearing my shirtwaister and cork wedges if the only one he ever saw looking at me was himself?

"Evil, incarnate in human nature," he went on. "As opposed simply to evil incarnate. Do you see the difference?"

But Rory McCloughlin had arrived with our plates of paella. When he'd seen us at the door, he'd scurried out from behind the counter, and smiled and said, "Good evening, Mr. Harding," and "Hello, Cressida, long time no see."

Everyone had turned to watch us then, everyone was

watching us still. I sat back on the cushions with my sangria. The last time I'd been here I'd rushed out and gone home on the bus and thrown my arms around Mr. Harding for the first time. But now I'd spoiled everything because of Campbell, everything, and there was nothing I could do to have things back the way they'd been before.

"Common criminals in charge," he said. "Can you imagine it?"

I shook my head.

"Picking and choosing with the power of gods." He drained his glass and poured us another. "Hunger," he said. "I don't think one can imagine hunger like that. The consuming obsession — the body, in fact, consuming itself."

"I know," I said miserably.

"Tell me," he said, "what did you come away with? What are you thinking now? Tell me."

The sangria was making my head swim. "I was thinking of my father."

"Ah." He put a hand over mine, which anyone could have seen. But he didn't seem to care or even to notice. "And I was thinking of you."

"Of me?" My heart gave a lurch.

"Well, of luck really, the haphazard nature of it."

Luck again. I was sick of the subject. And then suddenly I looked up and saw Mr. Ledson winding through the tables, making his way towards us.

"Harding!" he shouted, turning to pull a short blonde woman forward. She was wearing a pink maternity dress with a bow at the neck, and she had large, ugly freckles. "Meet Desirée," he said.

Mr. Harding put down his serviette and stood up for a

moment, but didn't take Mr. Ledson's hand. "We're in the middle of dinner, I'm afraid," he said. "Good evening to you both."

Mr. Ledson flicked at my shoulder. "This is the one I was telling you about," he said to Desirée. But I had shrunk back before he could touch me again. "See?" he said to her. "What did I tell you?" And he led her away without bothering to say good-bye.

"Well," said Mr. Harding, settling himself back down. "Where were we? Ah! Luck! Our old meeting ground."

*

Miranda was the one who used to massage Ma's feet, sitting where I was now, as silent as a slave. "Ma," I said, "why did Miranda say Mr. Harding was a dark horse?"

"If you're going to listen to Miranda you're more of a fool than you look. Press harder. That's better. How was the film tonight?"

"Fine. But you're the one who warned me about him."

"So what? Why don't you ask him if you want to know?"

"What I really want to know is what happened with you and Charles Harding."

Her foot stiffened in my hand. And then she pulled both feet away and sat up. "You're no good at this, you don't concentrate. Fetch me a brandy, would you? No ginger ale, please."

I got up and emptied what was left of the bottle into her glass.

"If I had it to do again," she said, holding out her hand for the glass, "believe me I would."

"That's an hypothesis that doesn't work, I'm afraid."

"Pure George Harding!" She gave one of her sarcastic laughs and swallowed the brandy in one gulp. "What I mean is, I only wish there'd been more men in my life like Charles Harding. A whole army of them. So what?" She glared at me. "So what?"

"All I really want to know is whether I'm my father's child," I said coldly.

She banged down the empty glass. "If George Harding is telling you otherwise it's because all he has to call his own is that twerp he fished out of the crèche!" She hauled herself up and went over to the drinks tray, standing there with the empty brandy bottle in her hand. "Whatever they say, Charles Harding was a gentleman, and I wish to God you were his child. But you aren't. You're just like your bloody father and always have been. And I hope you're satisfied now."

Chapter 33

The books were ready on the table, the tea tray as well. "Cressida," Campbell said, trying not to look at me, "I don't want what's between us to be furtive."

"What do you mean?" I stared down at the pencil he was twirling between his fingers. It was impossible that those fingers had touched me, impossible I had ever wanted them to.

"I don't want it to be shameful. That's not the way it is. It's not the way it should be."

He waited for an answer, but that was impossible, too.

"If I didn't love you, it would be different, I suppose."

"I've got to go to Oxford," I said quickly. It was all I could think of, and immediately, somehow, I knew it to be the truth. Suddenly Oxford was a way out of everything, even Mr. Harding. If I didn't get into Oxford I'd be stuck down the hill with Ma and Miranda and Bunch—everything I couldn't bear to go back to, not even for the few months I had left.

"I could get a job there, nearby perhaps." He blinked at me through his thick glasses. "I could do anything, you know. I don't have to teach."

I shook my head wildly. This was worse, far worse than landing up on the couch with him again.

"Please!" He made a grab for my hand and squelched it into his. Then he clutched it to his lips like a madman. "It was all my fault, I had the French letter at the ready for weeks. And I can't say I'm sorry either."

The gate bell rang and the dogs went roaring through the passageway, Phineas shouting after them. If it weren't for Campbell, everything would be normal. But there he was now, looking at me for an answer.

I pulled my hand away, and, before he could realise what I was doing, picked up my books and ran.

"Cressida!" He came after me, out into the courtyard. "Cressida!"

I bolted through the gate and across the driveway, nearly knocking into Phineas.

"Hau!" he said. "What the matter with you?"

I didn't answer, I just went through into the hall and out onto the verandah.

"Hello!" said old Mrs. Harding. "You're early today." She was in the rocker, listening to the afternoon concert on the radio.

I fell into a chair, my heart still thumping. What if Campbell came down the hill to see me? And Ma told Mr. Harding? Everything would be ruined, and I was the one to blame.

"That woman was here," said old Mrs. Harding. "She thinks I'm taken in. Well I'm not."

"Who?" I said. "What?"

"Oh, you know, we were there——" She waved her arm around.

"Mrs. Bourne-Thomas?" Just when I'd forgotten to think about her, here she was again. "Is she still here?"

"Gone again. Came Sunday, left Monday morning, just like that."

*

"Any more thoughts on *Night and Fog*?" Mr. Harding said. He was disappointed, I knew. He'd thought I'd be full of questions, full of comments, too. But Campbell was weighing down on everything now, even on my thinking. And it made it worse that everything else seemed the same—the sun striping in through the blinds, the dogs at our feet, the lesson over. There was the post, as usual, carried in by Phineas on the silver tray, and the ivory letter opener, the papers in neat piles around the clearing on the desk. But it wasn't the same, I'd squandered it all in one small half hour. And how could I be sure it wouldn't happen again, and not even with Campbell—with anyone, any fool at a bus stop offering to lift me up and carry me along, with nothing to hold on to, not even Mr. Harding?

"What's the matter? You're rather quiet today."

"I've been thinking about where I belong."

He sat forward. "Yes? How so?"

I shrugged. "Nowhere, I suppose."

"How so, I say?"

"Certainly not here."

He frowned.

"Not like Mrs. Bourne-Thomas I mean."

He sighed. "Look," he said, "she's a good woman, good company, too. And she needs a place to stay until she's settled. That's as far as I'm prepared to go. I could add that it's none of your business——" He stared down at his enormous hands, knitting them together. "Cressida, Cressida," he said, looking up again, "don't make this more difficult than it is already. Please!"

I could hardly breathe now under the weight of my secret. "Why not?" I said. "Why shouldn't I?"

But he'd already begun to put the books into a pile. Every day he had them ready for me, and after every lesson he ticked off another list on the timetable. "Go to Oxford," he said. "Do it for me if not for yourself."

"I will. I am. I mean I'll try. Maybe."

He twisted around to look at me. "If I said I'd wait for you, would that make any difference?"

My heart leaped and then sank immediately. "Difference to what?"

He stood up. It was my signal to go. "Where are you up to now in the Galsworthy? Perhaps you might find a way to bring him into one of your essays. What about the Boer War? From what I remember, he has a lot to say about it."

"What did you mean, you'd wait?"

He looked at his watch and began towards the door. But I stepped in front of him. I dropped my books and threw my arms around his neck, laying my cheek against his chest as I had the evening I'd come back from town on the bus.

For a moment he just stood there with his hands at his sides. But then he clasped them around me so tightly that, for a moment, I forgot all about Campbell, forgot about everything except that it was me he was going to wait for, me, me, me.

Chapter 34

But there was still Campbell. Since Tuesday I'd been waking up all through the night with the dread of him across my heart. So I sent a note up with Elias to say I had rehearsals after school and couldn't come for lessons anymore. And when I went in to see Mr. Harding, I told him the same thing. Ruth and I had cooked up the idea together on the way home, but all I'd told her was that Campbell was revolting, and I couldn't stand his awful English smell.

And then, on Saturday, just when I'd forgotten to worry about the whole thing, there was Ma saying, "There's a note for you from George Harding. Don't know why he doesn't just ring you up like a normal person." And I threw down my racquet and snatched the envelope off the kist.

Dear Cressida,
    I would be obliged if you would come to see me in my
study at 2 P.M. tomorrow.
    George Harding

"What's he want this time?" Ma said, coming through with her drink. There always seemed to be a drink now, they started just after tea, and sometimes in the morning before lunch. "I bought some wine for supper," she said. "Thought you might like a glass for a change."

I took the note to my room and closed the door. It was only five o'clock. He'd be back from riding, and the drinks tray wouldn't be coming in for another hour.

"Ma," I said, "I'm just going up to the big house. I won't be long."

"Well, tell him to send you back with Phineas, please. I don't want you walking in the dark."

I ran all the way up the hill, stopping only to catch my breath at the bottom of the verandah steps. And that's when I heard their voices, and her looping laugh. But just as I was about to turn around and leave, one of the dogs gave a little bark, and then they both came wagging down to find me. So it was hopeless, I had to go in, and there they all were, looking up in surprise.

Mrs. Bourne-Thomas jumped to her feet and held out her hands to me. "Cressida!" she cried. "What a lovely surprise! Look at you in your tennis togs! What a picture of youth and health!"

I glanced quickly at Mr. Harding, but he was wearing the hat and veil.

"Sit down, sit down," said Mrs. Bourne-Thomas. "Joining us for a drink? How lovely!"

I turned to Mr. Harding. "I can't come tomorrow," I said. "So I thought I'd come now."

"Very well." He pulled out his watch. "Would you excuse us, Mother? Elspeth? There's something I have to discuss with Cressida. Shouldn't take too long."

*

He stood at the table in his study, keeping his hat on.

"I've had rehearsals," I said quickly. "I meant to tell you."

"And I've had a visit from Edgar."

"Edgar?" My heart began to steady itself. Perhaps it was only Edgar, something for Edgar again.

He began to stalk up and down. And then suddenly he stopped and wheeled around. "He would have me believe he came out of friendship for the lovesick Campbell—at least that much I gathered from the stammering and stuttering." He gave one of his bitter laughs. "You didn't realise, did you, that your protégé fancied himself as Cupid?"

"Cupid?"

"Pandering. One of the lower crimes, you know. Remember Pandarus?" Another laugh. "But, really, it wasn't pandering at all. Were it not for his complete lack of grey matter, I'd consider him more of an Iago. He was here, essentially, to unseat you. And to do so by driving me to it. So you achieved something after all for all your pains with him, didn't you?"

I tried to understand, but the words jumbled around without meaning—Iago, Pandarus, Cupid. And yet, even so, I knew it had happened, it was over, and nothing would ever be the same again.

"And, of course, he succeeded. I summoned the little red-haired bastard on the spot, keeping Edgar where he was, right here, and what a pair they were, those two models of manliness on whom you chose to practice your charms! Red-faced as girls, each one blaming and denying until I told them I was throwing them both out, right out—and out they went this morning. Campbell's parting shot was an announcement that he intended to 'court' you anyway, for which, he was prepared to concede, he should have asked my permission in the first place, had you both not 'fallen into it'—his words, of course, not mine!"

He swung away furiously and folded his arms to stare out of the window, taking deep, rasping breaths until, at last, he said in a low voice, "It's the disappointment I find so hard to bear. Only days ago, a few little days, I was giving you assurances. And now this." He shook his head. "For what it's worth, I blame myself entirely."

"It's worth nothing!" I shouted, tears of rage and remorse coursing down my cheeks. "I'm sorry now, but what's the point of being sorry?"

He turned on me. "Sorry? Sorry? The housemaid's lament!"

But it was easy for him—easy to call me a housemaid and easy to take all the blame for himself. He could pick me up and put me down whenever he felt like it. But what about me? *I* was the one to blame, *I* was the one who should be allowed to be sorry for it, too.

"So what about *her*?" I shouted, pointing towards the verandah. "What about that stupid, bucktoothed, jolly hockey sticks stupid, stupid gymkhana cow out there! Who's to blame for *her*?"

"Control yourself at once!" He walked over to his chair and fell into it. "Sit down, Cressida!"

"I will not."

"As you please."

I was heaving now, gasping. "And why are you wearing your hat? Is that for her, too?"

Suddenly he exploded into a bitter laugh. "*Vanitas vanitatum*. Surely you realise how vain I am?"

"You told me you were a monster and you were right. You're hideous and disfigured and repulsive, and I hope you land up like my father!"

"Shall we call this a day?" He began to push himself up again. "I have a guest and I'd like to return to her."

"No!" I shouted. "You're the one who made me feel at home here, and I blame you for that! I can't feel at home anywhere else now, and I blame you for that, too! And for your bad temper! And your ludicrous vanity! And for using your scarred head as an excuse for everything you don't feel like doing! Other people have worse afflictions than yours, but they go out and do things! You just sit here, writing a book that's never going to be finished! Or you go to the stables, or to one of your mistresses! How would I know? And why should I care? Does *she* care?"

"Cressida!" he said, on his feet now. "I refuse to stand here, enduring your cheap rhetoric. Really, it's not worthy."

"I don't *care* what's 'worthy'! *I'm* not 'worthy' either— your word, not mine! I'm no better than my mother, am I? Or my sister? Or that mask you once made me wear? So why should I care?"

He didn't bother to answer, he just walked to the door and left it open for me to follow or not, it didn't seem to matter to him anymore. And when I came out into the hall, there was her laugh again from the verandah, and his joining in.

I stood for a moment, listening to them, trying to remember my first day here, and how much I'd longed to go home. But it was too late now. I wanted to stay. More than this, I wanted him to want me to stay. And it was too late for that, too, I'd spoiled everything myself. And I was the one being punished.

*

"Cressida?" Ma called when I came in. "Come out here, darling, you have a visitor."

I stood still for a moment.

"If you want a mineral, bring one from the fridge."

She was stretched along the swing seat, and Campbell was in a chair next to her. As soon as he saw me, he jumped to his feet and rushed over. He would have taken my hand right there if I hadn't snatched it away.

"What kept you up there all this time?" she said. "Bit thick on a Saturday, don't you think?"

I walked to the drinks tray to open a bitter lemon. A great rage had suddenly taken hold of my breathing, and I had to steady myself against the wall.

"Jock's staying for supper," she said merrily.

He came up to the drinks tray and stood behind me. I could feel his breath on my skin, smell the beer he'd been drinking.

"And what are these rehearsals you've been having?" she said, heaving herself up and on to her feet. "First I've heard of them."

"Cressida," Campbell whispered urgently. "What happened to you? What's the matter?"

I spun around. "Get out! I don't want to see you!"

"Cressida?" Ma struggled around. "What's the matter with you?"

He tried to catch at my hand again but I grabbed the bitter-lemon bottle and would have hit him with it if he hadn't stepped back, out of the way.

"He's blaming you as well?" he said, drawing himself up ridiculously. "Is that it?"

"Who's blaming whom?" Ma said merrily. She was cheered out of her usual Saturday night mood by a man to show off to, any man, even Campbell. "Why don't you go and change, darling?" she said airily. "Supper won't be for at least three quarters of an hour at the pace Elias goes, and you look as if you could do with a hose-down."

Chapter 35

For two months I didn't go near the big house. I didn't even go up the hill to wait at Ruth's gate. Anyway, Edwina Sloane was always there now, rehearsals or no rehearsals, and I didn't want either of them to think I cared. Only when Miranda came with the news that Mrs. Bourne-Thomas had moved into the old servants' quarters did Ma stop asking what had happened up at the big house and why. She'd heard, of course, that Campbell had been thrown out with two days' notice and Edgar along with him. They were both in a little flat down on the beachfront now, she told me. Mr. Harding had washed his hands of Edgar, even before he took his JC.

Night after night I lay on my bed, stupid with regret. And every day, when I came in, I ran to the kist in case there was a note from Mr. Harding. But there never was. The only news I had was from Ma, who'd had it from Miranda.

"Listen," Miranda said one day, pulling me aside. "What's the matter with you? You're not up the spout, are you? You can tell me, I won't tell Ma."

I shook my head, but suddenly I was in tears. Anything could bring them on these days, any mention of anything that could have happened at the big house. I put my arms around her neck and wept.

"Is it exams then?"

I'd heard Ma whispering to her. They were worried I was overdoing it, and would collapse, and let Mr. Harding down. And then he'd write me off, and, if he wrote me off, where would that leave the rest of them?

But the truth was that all I had to do was to read a paragraph in a set work, or go over a theorem, or look at my notes, and I'd begin to sink into a dark, thick sleep. It was more like death than sleep, heavy and dreamless, and when Ma woke me up for lunch or supper, I was still tired, and never hungry.

"Is it the work?" she said, patting my back as if I were a child.

I shook my head, miserable in my fraudulence. There was no one I could tell, not even Ruth. All she talked about now was matric and A levels for Oxford. She even dreamed about them, she said, horrible dreams in which she sat in the exam hall and had forgotten everything she knew, every single thing.

The day before exams began, an arrangement of flowers came from the florist. It was wrapped in cellophane and tied up with a bow.

"Here's a card," Ma said. "Let's see who they're from."

I opened the card and turned away to read it.

"Well?" she said over my shoulder. "Who?"

"It's from Mr. Harding. Here." I held it out to her.

"There! See?" She peered around me, into my face. "Now, what are you crying about? Here, here——" She pulled me to her, wrapping her arms around me. She smelled of brandy, I could hardly remember what she'd smelled like before. "So what do you care if he's counting on you? We're all counting on you! You're going to do the best you can, and if that doesn't suit him, he can take a running jump, flowers or no flowers."

I snorted hopelessly into her shoulder. "Oh Ma," I said. "It's too late now."

"Too late? For what?" Suddenly she pushed me away, looking hard into my miserable face. "You haven't got yourself into trouble, have you?"

I shook my head, sobbing hopelessly.

"Well then, what's all this rubbish? Take the flowers to your room. They'll cheer you up. And you should count on an early night tonight. I always used to have an early night before exams, and look where it got me in life! Ha!"

*

The first day in the exam hall I stared down at the English essay questions, wanting only to put my head down and sleep again. Girls had small china horses on their desks, and lockets, and snapshots of their boyfriends or their dogs. They were scratching away already, dipping and scratching, and chewing on their pens. But I just stared at the back of Fiona McKenzie's head, asking myself over and over why I should care if Mr. Harding was counting on me. Who did he think he was? Lord Muck on Toast? So why?

And then, suddenly, I woke up. For the first time in months I was awake, properly awake. I took off my watch and hung it on the desk as I always had, picked up my pen and began to go

down through the questions, crossing off the ones Mr. Harding had advised me to stay away from. "Not a story," he'd say.
"The stories are put in for the clots who can't sustain an ar-
gument. What you want is something you can get your teeth
into, pros and cons. What about this one, number 4: 'The
abuse of greatness is when it disjoins remorse from power'
(*Julius Caesar*). Comment and discuss'? That's the one I'd
choose if I were you."

I began to write. And every day after that, whether I was
translating Virgil or working out a theorem, it was his voice
asking the questions, his nod as I wrote out the answers. And
then, as I came out into the daylight with Ruth and Edwina,
suddenly he'd be gone again. And, walking with Ruth to the
corner, I didn't care about that either, because in a week, in
five days, in two, in three hours I'd be free of school forever,
and of Mr. Harding as well.

*

Crashing in through the front door on the last day, I stopped
dead at the sight of a note on the kist.

> *Dear Cressida,*
>   *I would be so pleased if you could come for tea with*
> *me in the little carriage house this afternoon at four. It's*
> *been such a long time since I saw you last, and now that*
> *exams are over, I do hope you can come. I've asked the*
> *boy to wait for an answer.*
>   *Yours,*
>   *Elspeth Bourne-Thomas*

I stared down at the card as if it were playing a trick on
me. All these past weeks, walking to or from exams, I'd been

settling into a sort of disdain for myself, and for any other woman who was fool enough to keep hoping for a note from a man, any man at all, but especially an old, scarred fool who wouldn't even take what he wanted. Who did he think he was anyway? And why would I care about Mrs. Bourne-Thomas or any other woman up or down the coast when I had my future to look forward to, whatever it was going to be?

*

I took the long way around so that I could go in through the back gate and avoid being seen by the big house. Standing in the alley again, listening to the shriek of the bell, I tried to remember the terror of those nights in the old servants' quarters. But it was impossible. Waiting there, breathing in the familiar stale damp of the passageway, I couldn't help feeling as if I were coming home.

Phineas came fussing down with the keys. "Hau, Miss Cress," he said, unlocking the padlock, "why you don't come by the front way no more?"

I laughed, listening to the echo.

"You still laugh for nothing," he grumbled, locking the gate behind me. "You too skinny now. You sick? Elias he don't make nice things to eat?"

A dog rushed up to greet me, and there was Mrs. Bourne-Thomas at the courtyard gate, saying, "Cressida! How good of you to come on the last day of exams!" She put an arm around my shoulders and led me inside. "It must be odd for you, coming back to this place."

But it wasn't odd, it was lovely. She'd changed everything around. The dining room was now the lounge, and the whole place was filled with faded floral linen and coir matting. It was lighter, too, with voiles on the windows and there were bowls of roses everywhere. I leaned over to smell one on the table next to me.

"Ah!" she cried. "I brought those down from upcountry. I had to go back there one last time to hand everything over, even my rosebushes. What a wrench that was!" She settled herself at one end of the couch and called out to the kitchen, "Lily, would you bring in the tea now, please."

And so I felt at home again for the first time in the months since I'd left. All those years that Mr. Harding had been veering me away from our world and into his own had done their work, and it was too late now to go back even if I wanted to.

As soon as Mrs. Bourne-Thomas had poured the tea and passed the plate of biscuits, she settled into the couch and said, "You must know, my dear, that I brought you here for a purpose."

I frowned as if I didn't understand, because really I wanted a few moments more of sitting there in her lovely old, worn chair, with a dog staring up hopefully at the cake. "You brought the dogs with you?" I said.

"Only Brutus. We had Cally put down the day before we left, she was riddled with cancer, alas. And, oh dear, he's mourning her terribly and so am I." She gave him a rub on his ears, but no cake.

And so we talked on a bit about dogs, hers and the ones we'd had ourselves, but quite soon she brought the conversation around to Mr. Harding's new puppy. He was from the same kennel as Brutus, she said, and before I could stop her she blurted out, "George Harding, as you must have realised, is the purpose behind my invitation."

My heart leaped, I couldn't help it, or stop the heat rushing to my face.

"There was a time when he was the only man I could imagine succeeding Nigel," she said. She ran her hands up and down her arms as if she were cold. Then she gave her toothy laugh. "He's the only man I know who's more impossible."

I pretended to smile along, but all I wanted now was to get her off the subject before it was too late. I looked desperately around for something to notice.

"If he hadn't been so impossible I might have worked it all out sooner, but it's hard to tell with him, you know. Even when he's not hiding behind that veil of his, he's quite adept at using those war wounds of his to mask any true feelings he might have. And, of course, there's his dreadfully bad temper."

I gave up and laughed. It was lovely, after all, to hear her talk about him as if I were the one who'd understand best.

"I'd always had the feeling that he was holding something back, but how could I possibly have imagined what it was? I'd thought it must be some tricky woman who wouldn't let go, something like that. Oh, my dear!"

I looked into my teacup. "There's nothing now."

But she hardly seemed to hear. "Mrs. Harding's another one. Quite mad for the most part, at least apparently so, and then there she is, sitting across the tea table, suddenly making complete sense of the whole thing. Do you think she puts it on a bit?"

"I don't know, I've never been able to work it out." I cast about for something to keep us where we were, even for a few moments longer. "She used to play the organ at St. Thomas's," I said.

"Yes, I know that, my dear." She gave me a steady look through her pale, pale eyes. "But you're the one I want to talk about. Forgive me this intrusion, but do you love him? Or are you just in love with him?"

I heard the words, I tried to understand that she had said them.

"What I mean is, have you lost sight of your future without him in it? Have you lost all sense of yourself in the first person singular?"

"I don't know," I said again, wanting now to throw my arms around her neck. "Really, I'm not sure of the difference."

"You're very young," she said. "I don't have to tell you he's more than twice your age. What you don't know, perhaps, is how very ill he's been these last few weeks." She seemed to be pleading for something, racing on before I could object. "The thing is, I'd like to move out next week, to my new little maisonette, and I was wondering—could you think of coming back, now that exams are over? For his sake?"

"Back here? To this place?"

"Oh, I don't know." She clasped her hands into her hair and seemed to be trying to tear it out of its ponytail. "I thought you might like to be out here? Independent? I can leave you the furniture if you can put up with it. It's not going to fit into the maisonette anyway." She looked over at me, her eyes watering over. "Do come back, my dear. You cannot imagine how much I have been longing for your exams to be over so that I could ask you."

I bit my lip. "I'll have to ask my mother," I said. But my heart was already wild at the thought of being back, here, with him, and her things all around me.

"If it would make it easier, I could certainly speak to your mother," she said.

"No, I'll ask her," I said quickly, standing up.

She stood up, too. "Perhaps she won't want you living on your own? I'm using the little corner bedroom down here, and the upstairs for storage, so you could have the whole thing if you wanted to. Or would she want you to have a companion? Edgar, perhaps? Well no, that wouldn't do, would it?" She looked around desperately. "What if I left you Lily? She could sleep upstairs, George doesn't mind about that sort of thing. How would that suit you?"

"I'll have to ask her," I said again, although I knew already that Ma would have to let me do whatever I wanted now, and if she knew the real reason, what did I care? I'd be back at Harding's Rest because Elspeth Bourne-Thomas loved the man who loved me so much that she'd give me anything I wanted just to make him happy.

Chapter 36

"Hau," said Phineas when I came into Mr. Harding's small lounge. "Why you don't knock? Master he don't like visitors."

I walked up to the couch, where Mr. Harding was lying in his dressing gown. "Why didn't you *tell* me?" I demanded. "Why didn't you at least send a note?"

When I'd told Ma that Mr. Harding was ill and I was going back to stay in the old servants' quarters, she was full of blame. Who did that Bourne-Thomas woman think she was, throwing in the sponge and expecting a girl of eighteen, barely out of school, to pick it up? Who did I think I was myself? Florence Nightingale? Joan of Arc? Why didn't George Harding just hire a proper nurse to look after him? It was ridiculous, but it was my life, and she only hoped he'd be paying me properly because she herself was up to her eyebrows, and now there was going to be Bunch to think of, too.

I sat down in the chair next to him and leaned forward. "What happened?" I said. "What have they done to you?"

He put down his book at last. "It comes off in a few weeks," he said. "How were the exams?"

If Phineas hadn't been fussing around, I'd have been able to take his hand and tell him everything now, everything.

He stared ahead of him. "Would you like me to arrange some piano lessons?"

"No, I certainly would not."

"Ha! Phineas," he said, twisting himself around with a grimace of pain. "I'll come down for tea this afternoon. Please tell the old Madam to expect us on the verandah."

"The verandah, Master?" Phineas hovered where he was.

"Certainly." Mr. Harding began to push himself slowly to his feet, and when Phineas ran forward to help, he said, "No. No, thank you. Off you go. I shall manage with Cressida's help."

Once he was standing, I could see that his whole torso was padded with bandages. "What did they do to you?" I said again.

"Oh, took some skin from here and put it there, long overdue. Would you pass me my hat, please? Thank you."

I watched him put it on with the usual ceremony, adjusting the angle, straightening the veil. There was a formality to him now that he'd never had before, not even that first day at Harding's Rest, when he'd tried to give me the bicycle.

"Ready?" he said. He began to move across the room, holding on to this and that as he went. I followed, longing for him to stop and take my hand. But he didn't, he hardly seemed to notice me at all. "My mother will be pleased," he said. "She's been asking about you daily."

"Could we talk after tea?" I said quickly, following close behind him. "Could we go to your study?"

But he just hung on to the banister, taking one step at a time. And then he made his way through the hall and out onto the verandah in silence.

I sat in my old seat, staring out at the garden as I always had. There was a heaviness in everything now, even in the new young dog chasing after the hadedahs on the lawn.

"Ah!" cried old Mrs. Harding. "She's back! See, Charles? See? Didn't I tell you she'd come back?"

I handed around the plate of jam tarts, glad to have something to do.

"Where's Elspeth?" said old Mrs. Harding, taking a jam tart. "Did you run her off?"

I laughed, I took her hand and kissed the loose skin. "She's moved to her maisonette," I said. "I'm here now."

"Oh, I'm glad about that, my dear. We're very glad, aren't we, Charles?"

He didn't answer, but if he asked me now what I dreamed of for my future I could have told him, it would be easy.

"Cressida," he said, looking up at last, "I'd like to see you in my study after tea. Can you spare a moment?"

*

"Why are you wearing the hat again?" I said, going to the window to look out at the old servants' quarters. It was lovely being back there, sleeping in my father's little room, with Lily coming in every morning to ask what I wanted for breakfast.

"Look," he said, "let's get one thing straight. It was I who was at fault. I might just as well have thrown you bodily into the arms of that little twerp! And to think that all the time it was Edgar I was worried about!"

"Edgar?" I turned to stare at him. "Please take that hat off so I can see whether you're joking."

When he didn't move, I went over myself and lifted it off. "What's really wrong with you?" I said, staring down at his pallid face.

But he'd reached for his pipe and was filling it from his pouch. "If you tell anyone I'm smoking," he said, "I'll send you home again."

I sank onto the carpet and rested my head against his leg. And I would have fallen asleep right there if he hadn't threaded his fingers through my hair and said, "What am I going to do with you now? When are the A levels?"

"I'm not taking them."

He puffed and puffed at the flame, and when Phineas knocked, he told him to go away. "Do you remember coming down here with the necklace my mother gave you?"

I nodded.

"Well, that's the way I feel about you."

"Like a thief?"

"Indeed, a thief. And so what, as you would say."

Chapter 37

For the next month it was back to the way it had been before. Every day I would go over to the big house for tea, and then to his study, and then to read to old Mrs. Harding before dinner. When we were alone, he'd invite me to sit in my usual chair, and please, he said, wouldn't I agree to have lessons again, it was driving him mad, hearing me fumble the same run every time in the "Allegro."

I laughed. He'd begun to read me bits of the book he was writing and would never finish. It was about everything he'd told me — the war and the flying, the concentration camp, the hospital, and also the boy he'd spent all those years looking for, the boy he'd managed to find. Ha!

Edgar was working in the Cotton Reel now. He'd turned up at the shop one day, wanting a job. He'd had holes in his shoes, Ma said, and Miranda had lent him money for a new pair. So now he was a glorified window dresser, poor thing, living like a church mouse after being so taken up and cared for. One thing you had to say for George Harding, she said, giving me one of her warning looks, when he wiped his hands of someone, that was certainly that.

And then, just as I was beginning to wonder whether he'd wiped his hands of me—just as I was about to give up myself because men were turning all the time to whistle at me in the street, boys at tennis were asking me to the beach or the pictures or for drives, and maybe I'd go after all because who did he think he was, keeping me cooped up like Rapunzel while he sat in his study, writing a book that would never be finished?— just then, I came in one afternoon and there he was, standing at the window with his arms held out to me. "To hell with Slatkin's warnings," he growled. "Come here to me this minute."

And so there we were again, clasped together, his face in my neck, his hands running over me like a blind person's. He folded me down right there, onto the pillows that were piled up against the wall for the dogs. And the strange thing was that it was nothing like that first night at Mrs. Bourne-Thomas's, nothing like anything I knew, not even Campbell, because it was another girl there, lying in my place, another Mr. Harding as well. He was still wearing his uniform, and behind him were the others, all of them smiling as they watched us, all of them waiting for the future.

*

He traced around my ear with a finger. "You'll move back in here now, with me. I can't risk having any more twits getting their hands on you."

Even in the gloom, I could see the blood glistening along

one of his scars. I looked up at his misshapen jaw, his eye, everything that had once so horrified me. "What did Dr. Slatkin say?"

"Ha! Slatkin!"

I rolled off the pillows and onto the zebra skin. It was warm from the sun. The whole room smelled wonderfully of animal skins and dogs and books newly painted for bookworm.

"I think I hear his car now. I could set my watch by that bloody man. Up, up, my girl, you must be out of here before he catches me and sends me back to Parklands."

"When do I move back?"

He sat up on one elbow and looked down at me. "Whenever you wish. Wherever you wish. I give up. To do otherwise would be to spit in the face of the gods."

*

That night I went up to his room with him after dinner. And the next day I packed my things and moved back into Mr. Charles's old room, everything just as I'd left it.

"What about the servants?" I asked over cognac a few nights later. Ma and Miranda had been asking for weeks what I was doing up there, now that school was over. Remember Sheila Forsdyck? Miranda had said, Cynthia's mother? Well, the whole town knew about her and George Harding, don't think they didn't.

"Bugger the servants!" he said. "I pay them not to see and not to hear."

I laughed. When he took me to the Playhouse for dinner, people gave each other looks. I knew what they thought, and they were right. His money had bought me, it had bought my whole family right from the start. And so what? I was paid for as surely as the servants or the watered silk on the walls of Mr.

Charles's room. "You haven't asked me about my future for a long time," I said.

He glanced at me over his glass. "You sound aggrieved."

"My mother thinks you're going to turn me into Sheila Forsdyck."

"Ah."

But the truth was that the only future I could imagine now was this, here, with him. If it was taken away again I would sink back in a minute into that dark, thick misery.

He sighed heavily. "I suppose there'll be no peace for us unless I offer them the blood sacrifice of marriage."

"Marriage?" Until Miranda had started on me, I'd forgotten all about his other women. So why should Sheila Forsdyck have the power to come along now and spoil all my happiness? "I don't care what they want! I just want everything to go on the way it is."

He looked tired suddenly. His face had whitened around the scars, his lips were pale. "I used to like to think of you as one of those wild children found curled up in a nest of leaves in the forest and brought to me by hunters for a bounty. Rousseau? Did we read Rousseau? I can't remember." He looked up and smiled. "She gave you your name in bitterness, you know, to punish you for the two men she herself had ruined."

I went over to his chair and sat on the arm. "I don't care about the future either," I said. "All I want is for things to go on like this."

He stroked my hand the way he stroked the dogs. "Nevertheless, we'll marry, and I shall consider my debt to them paid. I'll arrange for the magistrate to come to the house on Monday. But I don't want them anywhere near me from now on, do you hear? If you have to see them, you'll go down the hill to do so."

Chapter 38

If my father had been alive and I still stupid enough to think he could understand me, I'd have told him how Ma swayed and staggered now, hanging on to the furniture as she made her way across the room. Blaming her might have eased the tightness around my heart when I had to stop her from coming up the hill. Mr. Harding had to sleep in the afternoons, I told her, and he couldn't stand visitors. Sometimes he stayed in his room all day, I said, and had dinner up there on a tray.

And the strange thing was that I might as well have been writing the future myself, so truthful did it become. We'd had three months between the day I moved back into Mr. Charles's room and the day Mr. Harding collapsed on the floor of his study—three months during which I was so lifted up and carried along that all I waited for was the moment I could run down the passage to his room. There were mornings, too, and afternoons in his study. And once Phineas had come knocking there to say Campbell was at the front door, Ma had told him where to find me, and Mr. Harding rose like Jupiter and raged out into the hall, bellowing. And after that it was even better, because he couldn't bear to let me out of his sight. He didn't want to waste a minute of me, he said, not in the time that he had left. Losing the sight of an eye would be as nothing compared to that. And then he'd give out one of his terrifying laughs and pull me to him, so that I never knew what I was meant to take seriously and what I wasn't. And I didn't care a bit either.

And then, one day I came into the study and found him on the zebra skin, gasping. And after that he was confined to his rooms upstairs, and all I was allowed to do was to take his swollen hand in mine. There seemed to be too much flesh for the bones now, even on his fingers and along his jaw. The problem was that there wasn't enough air going to his heart, Dr. Slatkin explained to me. I should consider Mr. Harding a casualty of the war, he said, lucky only in that it had taken this long to happen. At half past five every day Dr. Slatkin came to give the daily injection, and I'd sit there, watching his small, pale hands as they filled the syringe.

"Your mother holding up down there?" Mr. Harding asked one day. He gave one of his damp grunts. "Managing to keep her at bay?"

I nodded. But if I could have sent her off on a ship for six months or a year, it would have been easier. When I brought this up with him, he just said, "Wait until afterwards." Until then everything was to go on as it was. There was to be no coyness about the situation either, he warned me, no special looks, no careful words, nothing whispered to the staff out of his earshot. He took my hand and brushed it across his swollen mouth. "To my mind, the Hindus have got something with their suttee," he said. "I cannot bear the thought of leaving you behind for someone else."

"But there is someone else," I said lightly. "I'm pregnant."

He reached for his pipe, which he smoked all the time, regardless of Dr. Slatkin. "I was wondering when you'd tell me. You surely realise that nothing is a secret in a house full of servants?" He looked up with his twisted smile. He smelled of the salve Phineas used on his chest. "I've instructed my solicitor accordingly. Come here, you silly widow, come and sit next to me, and tell me you regret nothing, even if you do."

*

"Selfish," Ma said, hanging a cigarette between her lips. We were sitting on the verandah, I couldn't keep her away after all. The first time she'd rung the front doorbell, I'd put my finger to my lips and led her out onto the verandah. And, since then, she'd been coming whenever she felt like it, trotting up the verandah steps just in time for tea. "You've always been selfish," she said. "And now that you've got what you want, to hell with the rest of us."

"Ma," I said, "Mr. Harding is very sick."

"'Mr. Harding' this, 'Mr. Harding' that!" she spat out. "Why can't you just call him 'George' like a normal wife?"

I gave up. If I told her I never called him "George," not even to his face, she'd break into one of her vulgar, pealing laughs. And then, the next thing, she'd be on the phone to Miranda, both of them making fun of him. All these years he'd been asking me about my future, and here it was. It had slipped in so quietly with our blood sacrifice that no one, not even I, had seen it coming.

And then suddenly I heard the lift clang. Mr. Harding had had it put in near the back stairs to spare himself the indignity of being carried down by Phineas. Only Phineas was allowed to push his wheelchair or to help him in or out of it, or to do all sorts of things that everyone else was shut out from, even me.

"I thought he didn't come down till tea time?" Ma said quickly, gathering up her cigarettes and lighter. In her haste she knocked the ashtray to the floor and crouched down to pick up the pieces.

"Leave it!" I said. "I'll get someone to sweep it up."

She started scrambling to her feet. There was blood on her finger, and she wiped it wildly on her skirt.

"Ma!" I said, "*Sit* down! Now!"

But she was staring at the doorway. They were there already, Phineas, and Mr. Harding in the wheelchair.

"Hello, George," she said.

He was wearing his hat. He wore it all the time now. "Phineas," he said, "I'll go to my study. Cressida, if you could join me there for a minute, please?"

"I'll come later," I said. "My mother's come for tea."

Even Phineas looked up then, staring from me to Ma and back again.

She brushed furiously at the ash on her skirt. She knew she was unwanted here. It was why she kept coming back, just to make sure. Well, now she was sure, and what could I do but fight for her?

"Ma," I said, "would you kindly sit down?"

She glared at me. "There was a time when your husband was glad to see me. You should ask him about it sometime." She was wearing the Indian sandals she kept for around the house, and her nail polish was peeling, her hair was unwashed.

"Muriel," he said in his careful, cold voice, "kindly leave my house immediately."

I walked around her chair to stand between them. "Phineas, please go and order tea."

Beads of sweat had broken out on Phineas's upper lip, but I could see him relax his grip on the handles of the wheelchair. He knew as well as I that it wouldn't be long now, and then there'd be his children to think of, his wife and himself as well.

"I didn't mean to intrude," Ma said with a meekness that didn't suit her. But she herself had to look to her future now. What would become of her if Mr. Harding threw me out? What would become of all of us?

Mr. Harding wiped a hand across his face. Small coughs began to stutter out of him.

"It's unreasonable," I said to him quietly. "You know how unreasonable it is."

But he wouldn't look up, and when Phineas said, "Master? Must I take you to the study?" he wouldn't answer then either.

"Well then," Ma said, "off I go. Bye, darling!"

I turned to watch her walk down the verandah steps. Elephant Walk was what she'd taken to calling the hill between us. "Run along," she'd say. "Scuttle back to him up Elephant Walk."

"Bye!" she sang out as the gate clicked shut behind her.

I listened to her sandals slapping down the pavement on the other side of the hedge. "Would you like some tea?" I said to Mr. Harding. "Please. For my sake."

Chapter 39

"You a good girl," Phineas whispered when I came into the little living room after dinner. "You honour your mother, you honour your father."

I went through to sit in the chair next to Mr. Harding's bed. All through tea he'd said nothing, answered no one, and refused to eat or drink. I was the one who'd had to call Phineas to wheel him away again, and after they'd gone and old Mrs. Harding had taken my hands in hers and said, "What is it, my dear?" I'd burst into tears and run up to my room and out onto the verandah.

A storm was coming in, so much the better. There was no future to look for out there for me anymore, it was too late for that. I stretched out along the wall and closed my eyes. Why hadn't he just taken what he'd wanted the way other men did, even Campbell? We could have had more than just these measly three months if he hadn't wasted all those years, asking and asking when I couldn't even hear him. Ruth said it had been that way all through history, old men taking young girls for wives. She was leaving for Oxford soon, and I was glad I wasn't going with her. I was nearly nineteen, but I felt too old for Oxford, too old for everything except Mr. Harding.

"Cressida," he said softly, "you'll find a friend in Elspeth." He spoke slowly, gasping for breath between words.

I took his swollen hand. "Do you want to see her? Shall I ask her to come tomorrow?"

He put a hand on my stomach. "Still sick?"

I shook my head. Ma said everyone thought I must have blinded and deafened him because how else could I have got a man like George Harding to marry me. How? And it wasn't hard to see how things would go on and on from here. As soon as the funeral was over they'd be marching up Elephant Walk whenever they felt like it, Ma and Miranda, and Bunch as well. As far as they were concerned they'd have a right to me, and when they found out about the baby it would only make things worse.

He groped towards a hanky on his bedside table, and then broke into a cough, heaving and gasping.

I tried to lift him as I'd seen Phineas do. But just as I was about to call out for help, there was Phineas himself, creeping in like an apparition. "Out now, Miss Cress," he said, waving me off.

I stood at the door, watching as Phineas lifted him and clapped him on the back. He was trying to say something to Phineas, trying to gasp it out quickly before the next cough took hold of him. But Phineas just went on clapping until the coughing subsided. And then he laid him back down, smoothing and tucking in the sheets, deaf in the way he'd always been deaf when he didn't want to listen.

A crack of thunder broke, and Phineas switched on the bedside lamp.

"Cressida!" Mr. Harding called out as soon as Phineas was gone. "You still there?"

I went up to the bed and took his hand again. It was like a dead thing. If it hadn't been his I'd have flung it away in disgust.

"I wanted to free you," he said. "I've always wanted to free you. It's been like a disease."

"Free me?" Already there were phone calls from Miranda, asking in her little voice if she could have a little loan to tide her through the month. There was Bunch, too, and Edgar. He couldn't afford the rent on his little flat anymore, Ma kept telling me, and Miranda said she should move him into my old room. But when I told her you had to look out for Edgar, he was a snake, she just laughed. I'd had all the luck in the family, she reminded me, and I shouldn't let it blind me to the needs of others.

"It won't be easy," Mr. Harding said vaguely. He was drifting off now, I'd learned to tell the signs. "I gave up on Oxford, you must give me that."

I looked into his face, seeing past the distortion of flesh to the furious man I'd seen that first day in his study. I loved returning to the terror of that afternoon, the way he'd freed me from Mrs. Arbuthnot's hand clawing into my shoulder.

"Bring me a glass of water, please. And the brown bottle in the medicine chest. Fetch them now, there's my darling." He spoke in a whisper and with great effort.

I brought them to him, showed him the bottle, laid the glass of water next to his bed. He put his hand out for me to take. It was heavy and hot, and I knew he wanted me to leave.

"There are things I have to say!" I said desperately. "To tell you! Please!"

But his eyes were fluttering. "Go out now," he said. "Leave me. Close the door."

I took off my shoes and crept out, closing the door silently behind me. I slid past the sewing room, where Phineas was snoring already, and made my way out of the north wing and along the passage to my room. I stood there for a long time, staring out at the storm. It was perfect, thunder and lightning and the rain washing across the verandah. And then I climbed into bed with my clothes on, shivering despite the heat.

Coda

It is ten years now since the night Mr. Harding killed himself. Phineas was the one who lied for me. He told them I'd gone to bed before he did, that he'd closed the door because the Master had told him to. It was he who coaxed old Mrs. Harding into the wheelchair for the funeral, and when she asked for the fourth time where we were going and why she was wearing her good pearls, he was the one who said, "Master George he die. We got to go to the funeral now."

As far as Phineas was concerned the funeral itself was a paltry affair, worse even than my father's. "Hau, Miss Cress," he said, "shame for just cold meat and salad. What the Master he think?"

"The Master hated a fuss."

But Phineas just shook his head. "I make some honey loaf?" he said. "I make some jam tart and trifle?"

And from then on, that's how it went—Phineas asking,

Phineas doing what he thought should be done. But when I suggested that he bring his family to stay in the servants' quarters, I'd fix it with the authorities, he just shook his head vigorously. No good, he said, too many tsotsis in town, too many bad womens as well. It was Ma who pointed out that he had women in town already. She'd seen him leading one through the back gate after church all those years before, and then out again early the next morning.

As soon as the funeral was over, Ma put our house on the market, good riddance to bad rubbish, she said. The so-called improvements that Ledson had made were so cheaply done that she'd have had to lay out a fortune just to get rid of the white ants. So now a developer was taking it over. He was going to put on another story and turn it into maisonettes. Maisonettes were the way of the future, she said, she'd have bought one herself if I hadn't persuaded her to move back into the carriage house with Bunch and Edgar, and to put her money in the bank.

As soon as she was there, she began to grumble about being relegated to the role of glorified housekeeper, seeing to the meals and so forth. Perhaps I'd like to move her off the premises altogether, she suggested? Perhaps I'd like her out of the way when that Bourne-Thomas woman came over for tea? Ma was jealous of Elspeth Bourne-Thomas, she was jealous of everyone who came near me, even Phineas. He, after all, had let her find out for herself that I was going to have a baby. And when the baby was born and I told her I was naming him Malcolm, after my father, she said it was clear I was still bent on punishing her, and she supposed she'd just have to bear it, what else could she do, a woman without means in the middle of her life?

But she did have means, Mr. Harding had seen to that, and

for Edgar as well. And when I told her I was going away for a year on a ship with Elspeth Bourne-Thomas, and the nurse, and the baby, that's when she suggested that she and Edgar might come along for a lark. He was keen on seeing his old friend Guy again, she said, and, as for her, a trip overseas was long overdue.

So I told her at last I didn't want either of them, I wanted to go on my own. And that's when she said I could stuff off, she was going to use the little she had to rent a flat on the beachfront, leaving Bunch and Edgar up there with me. And if I wanted a housekeeper or a butler to hold the fort every time I felt like waltzing off on a ship like Odysseus, I could just ask them. Ha ha she didn't think.

*

As it turned out, I had as happy a year as I could have imagined, and by the time we came home I was married to Guy Bourne-Thomas. Mr. Harding would have hated the sight of Guy's arm around my shoulders, Guy going through the house room by room, his blonde hair falling into his eyes as he sorted and catalogued, setting things aside for restoring, cleaning, painting. He would have hated the sight of Edgar, too, scurrying behind Guy like a little dog with his notepad and pen. Guy never tired of going over and over things with Edgar, teaching him so patiently that sometimes I stopped to watch. But then Edgar would catch sight of me and stop dead, terrified. I had always terrified Edgar, I explained to Guy. Everything seemed to terrify him, even the house itself.

Guy shook his head, baffled. He had always loved this house, he said. It was the most glorious example of an era so soon to be past that we should do everything we could to preserve it, even turning it over to the university, perhaps, when the children had grown up and gone away.

And so something was to go to the university after all, although it was never going to be me. Whatever I was to learn I'd find out for myself, and always there'd be Mr. Harding's voice behind me, asking the questions, coaxing out the answers, his hand still warm in my hair.

Acknowledgments

For the gift of time, peace, and a beautiful place in which to write, I thank the Corporation of Yaddo, the Bogliasco Foundation, The European Centre of Translation—Literature and Human Sciences, and Civitella Ranieri. Without the friendship, intelligence, loyalty, and encouragement of Ann Patty I would be lost. And to Jennifer Rudolph Walsh, darling friend and fierce protagonist, I owe much more than this book. Thank you.